ABOUT THIS BOOK

Welcome to the darker, sexier side of Havenwood Falls that many residents never speak of publicly, but most likely enjoy in secret. Venture into the SIN MC, the VIP rooms of Silk nightclub, and behind other closed doors, where you'll discover passion, unusual penchants, and just how far some will go for love. Hold on to your panties, because it's time to ride . . .

Mavis LeGrand had always suspected her grandfather was a little off, and when he suddenly moved them to a remote town in Utah, her suspicions rose. Nevertheless, she lived a typical life—high school, friends, and eventually college in the small but safe town he'd chosen. But when she finds his journal after a life-altering accident, she learns the hard truth—her grandfather isn't human, and neither is she.

She also discovers his plans to use her power in the evil scheme he's been arranging since her infancy.

Knowing her very existence depends on him never finding her, Mavis makes her escape and hitches a ride with the devilishly handsome half incubus, Cameron DeSalle. Despite her initial trepidation, she instantly feels a connection with him and believes him when he says he'll do everything in his power to protect her.

Mavis finds herself falling for Cameron, the ice in her veins melting away with every heated look and stolen kiss. But whether Cameron feels the same desire for her or it's his incubus nature bringing them closer, Mavis isn't sure. The only thing she knows for certain is until they defeat her grandfather, they'll never have a happily ever after.

HAVENWOOD FALLS SIN & SILK BOOKS

Taming the Beast by Nadirah Foxx

Plans Laid Bare by J.D. Nelson

Shift of Fate by Victoria Escobar

Stolen Wishes by Victoria Flynn

Damned Allure by Justine Winter

Savage Salvation by Kristie Cook

Dark Seduction by Michele G. Miller & R.K. Ryals

Soul Laid Bare by J.D. Nelson

Stray With Me by E.J. Fechenda

Chase the Flames by Desiree Lafawn

Flirting With Death by Nadirah Foxx

Also try the signature line, Havenwood Falls, the historical paranormal line, Legends of Havenwood Falls, and stories from the local supernatural college in Sun & Moon Academy.

Stay up to date at www.HavenwoodFalls.com

ALSO BY J.D. NELSON

PLANS LAID BARE

A HAVENWOOD FALLS SIN & SILK NOVELLA

JD NELSON

To Nels, always Nels

PROLOGUE

"Shit! Shit! Shit!" I muttered, frantically shoving the clothes from the laundry basket into my backpack. I had to do this faster. "Think! Think, Mavis! You can do this!"

I blew out a breath, trying to calm myself enough to concentrate on what I needed to do next. Everything was moving so fast. I couldn't grab hold of the thoughts racing through my head. How could this be happening to me?

Stopping, I closed my eyes and took a deep, cleansing breath. I needed clarity, focus. And I needed it yesterday.

I opened my eyes. Money. I was going to need lots of money.

Straightening the room as I went, I stopped at the door to look for anything out of place. The room was messy, as usual, but not I-packed-my-whole-world-in-three-minutes messy. He was used to seeing this level of clutter.

This will work, I thought. *It has to work.*

Throwing my backpack over my shoulder, I set out at a brisk pace, making a beeline to the jar of mad money he kept on top of the refrigerator. As tempted as I was to take it all, I didn't. I had to make sure nothing was amiss. If anything was different, if anything caught his eye, he would know, and he would come for me. That couldn't

1

happen. Having a decent head start would mean the difference between life and death.

CHAPTER 1

*J*ran until I couldn't run anymore. My feet ached. My mouth was as dry as the Sahara Desert. My clothes were dirty and torn from ducking behind trees and diving into ditches in blind, terrified panic. And I was tired. We're talking the weary-to-the-bone kind of tired. The kind of exhaustion you feel when you've been down with the flu for three days and try to do something normal . . . like breathe.

I smiled bitterly as I kicked a rock, listening to it skitter down the pavement into the darkness beyond. I knew I would never have to worry about something as mundane as the flu again. Because, as of two hours earlier, I had learned the truth about myself. I'd never been normal. I was as far away from ordinary as I could be. I was an ice demon.

Yes, an ice demon. Me, Mavis LeGrand, college graduate, ex-cheerleader, and high school debate club president, a demonic entity.

Of all the absurd things I thought could happen to me, finding out I was a creature of Hell hadn't even been on the list. The mere idea was ludicrous. Before this afternoon, my life had been boring. There'd been no excitement, no surprises. And no one could have had a more idyllic upbringing than I had. Sure, the thing pretending to be my grandfather had been a little cold and creepy, but a demon with a propensity for evil? Not in a million years would I have suspected him of that.

I snorted to myself, almost delirious in my exhaustion. As if any of that stuff still mattered. That fake life was over. It didn't exist anymore. And it never would again.

The faint glow of headlights in the distance pulled me out of my misery and set my heart racing. Darting to my right, I dove headfirst into a deep and, thankfully, grassy ditch and prayed that the vehicle wouldn't stop. I'd come so far. I couldn't let my grandfather find me after everything I'd been through tonight.

I tried to hold my breath as the sound of the tires grew closer, but a sharp sob tore out of me on its own volition when I heard the telltale squeak of the brakes and a door opening. All the effort, all the ridiculous abuse I'd put my body through—it was for nothing. He'd found me. My grandfather had found me.

"I'm not one to pry into someone else's business," an unfamiliar voice drawled, "but I've got to tell you, when I saw you take that Olympic dive into the drainage ditch, I had questions. Mainly, what the hell is that little blond woman doing?"

With tears streaming down my face, I sat up to see a pair of black boots come to a stop in the gravel in front of me. Though I couldn't make out his features with his truck's headlights shining so brightly behind him, I knew he was smiling down at me. I could hear humor in his deep, gruff voice.

"Aw, coach, I'm just practicing for the next meet," I told him, damn close to hyperventilating. "We're going to bring home the gold this year!"

The man's sharp bark of a laugh made me jump.

"You do that now," he said.

I grinned. "I'll give it my best shot."

"I never had a doubt. But before you do that, why don't I give you a ride somewhere. Where're you headed?"

"It doesn't matter," I said truthfully. "Anywhere that's out of town."

"Well, then, you're in luck. I happen to be heading in that direction."

I pursed my lips, weighing my options. Hitchhiking with a stranger was crazy. I knew it. He knew it. Everyone knew it. But the urge to take him up on his offer was overwhelming. The man did seem genuinely concerned by my ditch antics.

But still, my grandfather didn't raise a fool.

"How do I know I can trust you?" I asked him, narrowing my eyes.

"You don't. But riding with me is better than risking a rattlesnake bite every time a truck comes down the road, right? And I promise to behave myself, so what do you have to lose?"

I had to admit, even in early October, he had a point about those snakes. I didn't know how many more times I could repeat my swan-dive-into-questionable-ditches routine without suffering serious injury.

"Okay," I said finally. "Thanks."

Crouching down, he reached out a hand to help me up. "Here, let me give you a . . . shit." He stood up quickly. "Get down. Someone's coming."

Lying flat, I watched the man step closer to the edge and move his hands to his fly.

"What are you doing?" I hissed.

"Saving your ass," he whispered. "Now lie still. They won't stop if they think I'm taking a piss."

Closing my eyes, I concentrated on the crunch of crisp leaves as the vehicle slowly approached.

"Evening," I heard my would-be savior call. "Do you want to hold it for me or something?"

I trembled uncontrollably as a scolding, laced with obscenities, erupted from the driver. It was him. My grandfather had found me.

"Don't let him see me," I whispered as the car sped off. "Please."

"Come on, then," he said, squatting down to reach for me. "Hurry up."

I took the hand he offered and shouted, "Oh!" when a warm jolt of electricity traveled up the length of my arm.

"Sorry," he said apologetically. "I wasn't expecting you to be an immortal," he explained. "Humans can't feel that. I was trying to put you at ease."

"Put me at ease? What just happened?"

"I'm a cambion," he said simply, as if that would explain everything.

"A what?"

"I'll tell you in the truck." He opened the passenger side door. "We need to get going, in case he doubles back."

I nodded and quickly brushed the debris from my clothes, not knowing what to think about his revelation. Was a cambion a demon like myself or something different? Was he dangerous? Did that even matter? Whether he killed me or my impostor grandfather did, I was still one dead demon chick.

Finally, I decided to throw caution to the wind and climbed into the truck. Buckling my seatbelt, I waited for him to get in on the driver's side before I blurted out, "I'm an ice demon."

"Those are rare," he replied, nonplussed.

"Are they? Do you know anything about them?"

He chuckled and cranked his truck. "Don't you?"

I shook my head. "No. I just found out I was a demon, oh . . ." I checked my nonexistent watch. "About two hours ago. I'm hoping the learning curve isn't steep."

"What's your name?" he asked, whipping the truck around to head for the interstate.

"Mavis LeGrand."

He nodded, leaning over to switch on the interior light. "I'm Cam, Cameron DeSalle. Pleased to meet you."

I blinked a few times, letting my eyes adjust to the sudden brightness. Then I lost my power of speech. My Good Samaritan was a dark angel in tight blue jeans.

A furrow appeared between his brows. "Are you okay, Mavis?"

"Y-yeah, I just didn't expect . . ." I threw my hands up. "Cameron, you're like, crazy hot. You know that, right?"

He laughed. "Yes, but I don't think anyone has ever told me quite so bluntly."

"I'm sorry." I groaned, covering my face and lamenting my idiocy for a moment until I remembered how filthy my hands were and jerked them away from my face so fast, I accidentally hit one against the dash. When I looked up, nursing my aching hand to my chest, Cameron was staring at me with surprised amusement.

"You are a very entertaining ice demon," he told me.

"Thank you. And I'm sorry." I laughed. "It has been a day, and after everything else, I wasn't expecting someone so . . ."

"Attractive?" he asked. "Sexy? Irresistible?"

I gestured at his square jaw, thick black hair, and kind honey-brown eyes that would make any woman's panties melt right off. "Well, yeah. I mean, look at you, Cameron."

"Call me Cam," he reminded me.

"Okay. Cam the cambion, you're a regulation hottie. What's up with that?"

He groaned. "Come on, Mavis. A *Mean Girls* reference? I thought you were better than that."

"Then you thought wrong, because I'm really not," I told him, feeling almost hopeful for the first time since my world fell apart. "Now spill. What's it like to walk around with a mug like that twenty-four seven?"

"What's it like to walk around looking as pretty as you do?" he shot back.

"First off, don't even; I'm not the same caliber as you," I said. "And second, quit deflecting. I want an answer. Do women follow you around like the Pied Piper or what?"

He blew out a very put-upon sigh and leaned back in his seat. "Women are often attracted to me, yes."

"Knew it," I said smugly.

"It's not as if I want them to," he said, suddenly sitting upright. "I don't have a choice. My father is an incubus."

I blanched. "An incubus? Like, the steal-souls-by-having-sex kind of incubus I've read about in books?"

He gave me a winsome smile. "Yes. And that is a very accurate description."

"Do you do that? Steal souls, I mean."

He answered without the slightest bit of guilt. "Yes, but don't worry. You have nothing to fear from me."

"And why is that?" I asked, more than a little wary after his frank admission.

Cameron's dark eyes scanned my face for a moment before he turned his attention back to the road. "Because you don't have a soul, Mavis."

"I don't have a soul?" I asked in disbelief.

He shook his head. "Not that I can detect, no."

I sat back against the seat in stunned silence, wondering how this could be my life. Everything had been so boringly normal the day before. It was like I woke up in the twilight zone.

"I'm sorry," he said sheepishly. "That must have been a shock for you. I wasn't thinking."

"It's okay," I told him, my eyes welling up with tears again. "There's nothing to be done about it. It is what it is."

"There's a bottle of water in the glove compartment," he offered, looking at me as if he didn't know what to do about the dirty, tear-stained mess next to him.

Numb, I nodded and woodenly reached for the latch. I didn't know what to do about me, either.

"You're going to be okay," he said gently. "You're still the same demon you were yesterday. You just didn't know it yet."

I closed my eyes and inhaled deeply through my nose, holding it in a few seconds before exhaling. "Thank you, Cameron."

His expression turned serious as he clicked off the light. "It's no problem, but you do realize you're going to have to tell me what's going on, don't you? Obviously, you're in some trouble."

I pressed my lips together. As important as this was, it was hard to say something when you didn't want to hear it out loud. Hearing it out loud made it real. I wasn't ready for real yet.

"Come on," he urged. "I'm invested in this thing now. I want to help you. And that means I have to know who you're running from, so I can keep both of us safe."

"Okay," I said, straightening in my seat to face him. "I'll tell you, but only because I need help. And Cameron, if you're offering it to me, I'm going to take it. I don't have a choice. I don't think I can do this on my own." I blew out a shaky breath. "So, are you sure you want to help me?"

"I am," he said without hesitation. Then he pulled to the side of the road and shifted the truck into park. "Tell me how to help you, Mavis."

Wrapping my arms around myself, I sank back into my seat, staring at the road stretching out in front of us. "I'm running from my grandfather."

"Your grandfather?" Cameron asked incredulously. "Why on Earth would you do that?"

I met his gaze. "Because he's not my grandparent. He's not even related to me. He's an ice demon, and he's planning on killing me."

CHAPTER 2

I thought Cam would insist I get out of his truck—that he'd leave me in his dust. But he didn't. Instead, he asked, "Did you just say your pretend grandfather is planning to kill you?"

I nodded, trying hard to keep eye contact. "Apparently, I'm the Exitium Daemonium."

His eyes widened. "The Exitium Daemonium? Like *the* Exitium Daemonium? Are you serious?"

"One hundred percent serious," I told him glumly.

"So the prophecy is true," he said, more to himself than me.

"I guess. I know less than nothing about the whole thing. What do you know about it?" I asked.

"Same as any demon knows. The Exitium Daemonium will bring death and destruction to demonkind."

I rolled my eyes. "Look at me, Cam. Do I look like I'm going to bring death and destruction to demonkind?"

"No, you look like an extremely filthy librarian."

"I rest my case."

"How did you find out?"

"I had an accident today."

"Like a car accident or an I-killed-a-demon type of accident?"

As his words sank in, my heart began to thump wildly. "Do you really think I can kill a demon?"

He laid a hand on top of mine to stop my fidgeting with the cap on the water bottle. "Mavis, if what you're saying is true, you're the ultimate in demon destruction."

"That's the thing," I said, ignoring the zing of energy that shot through me when he touched my skin. "I don't feel like hurting any demons. I feel stronger and keep having cold flashes since the accident, but I'm not having homicidal urges or anything."

"I think you'd better start at the beginning."

"Okay." I took a deep breath. "Late this afternoon, I fell down a huge flight of stairs at the public library, and when I was rushed to the hospital and x-rayed for suspected broken ribs, they found this weird anomaly that looked like it was encasing my heart, so they did an MRI."

"What did they find?"

"Nothing from the MRI. The machine blew up the second they turned it on. The explosion should have killed me, or at the least, burned me, but nothing happened. During all the confusion, smoke, and sirens, I ran."

"And since then you've felt stronger and have been feeling cold?"

I nodded. "I ran all the way from just south of Provo and never broke a sweat."

His mouth dropped open. "But that's forty miles from here. You've been jumping into ditches for forty miles?"

"Or ducking behind trees, or mailboxes, or cars. Whatever kept me from being seen."

He shook his head in wonder. "So, this anomaly, it had to be a throttle of some sort, right?"

"A throttle? Do you think that's what it was?"

"I do. There's no other way you wouldn't have noticed by now your ability to manipulate the cold. Did you get a chance to see the anomaly on the x-rays?"

"Unfortunately, yes. I'm pretty sure it's going to haunt my dreams."

"What did it look like?"

"Something diamond-shaped with runes engraved into it," I answered. "I couldn't tell what it was made of, though."

"Do you know anything about the runes that were on there?"

"See, that's where this whole thing got even more freaky. When I was little, I stumbled across a set of journals that had the same runes on them in my grandfather's study. He was pissed when he saw me playing with them, so the memory sort of sticks out to me. As soon as I saw the x-ray, I knew there had to be a connection, and I knew I needed to find those journals."

Cam looked suitably impressed. "And did you find them?"

I stared down at his big hand still covering my small ones. It was warm, comforting, and sending a flow of energy through me so filled with slow-burning desire, I almost hoped he'd never move it.

"Mavis?" he prompted.

"I did sneak into his library to read them," I said, finally meeting his eyes. "But I wasn't able to get past the first one before I knew I had to get out of the house. I had to get as far away from him as possible. Whoever he is, he isn't my real grandfather. He stole me from the underworld when I was an infant. He has plans to . . . He plans to . . ." I broke off, not able to finish the sentence. The horror of what I'd read was too fresh to talk about just yet.

He squeezed my hand briefly, then turned his attention back to the road. "There's a cheap motel up ahead," he said, throwing the truck into gear. "We can figure out what to do next once we're there."

I sighed in relief. "Thanks, Cam."

"Trust me. I'm doing this for me as much as I'm doing it for you. We can't let you fall into the wrong hands."

I frowned. "You say that like I'm some sort of weapon."

He caught my gaze as we passed under a streetlamp. "Not some weapon, Mavis, *the* weapon. I have to protect you in any way I can. There's no choice here. My own immortal life could depend on your safety."

I swallowed hard and nodded my acquiescence. Cam was right. I just hoped like hell my new friend would be up for the task.

~

CAMERON PARKED his truck behind the Starlight Motel after making a pit stop at an all-night burger place. He left me eating a large order of fries and slamming a thirty-two-ounce soda while he checked us in. Five minutes later, we were inside room seventeen, staring awkwardly at each other.

The room was clean and tastefully decorated with the latest in hotel chic. And me? I was incredibly dirty and feeling filthier by the second.

"I'm going to shower," I told him, grabbing my backpack. "I'll be right back."

"Take your time," he said through a mouthful of bacon cheeseburger. "Do you need clothes? They might be a little big, but I think I have a pair of sweats and a T-shirt that will do."

I had a few moments of pure yearning as I looked over to the overnight bag he was pointing to. What would it be like to be warm and wrapped up safe with his manly scent all over my body?

"Mavis?"

My cheeks heated up with a blush, and I sputtered, "Thank you. But I packed extra clothes in my backpack. I'm all right."

He nodded and helped himself to a handful of my uneaten fries. "Have a nice swim, then."

Once inside the bathroom with the door locked behind me, I twisted on the shower taps and braced my arms on the vanity.

"You will not think about how hot he is," I told the wistful, gray-eyed girl in the mirror. "You will ignore the unbelievable hotness."

And I did. For the next half hour, I didn't think about anything but the methodical process of washing the dirt from my body. When I was squeaky clean and feeling a hundred pounds lighter, I toweled off, brushed my teeth and hair, and dressed in clean yoga pants and a V-neck sleepshirt. I stepped out of the steamy bathroom looking and feeling like a new demoness.

Cameron had made himself at home while I showered. Lounging on the bed in gray sweatpants and a Smashing Pumpkins T-shirt, he was just putting down his cell phone and picking up the remote to flip through the channels on the ancient TV when I walked into the bedroom.

"Feel better?" he asked, barely glancing up.

I sat cross-legged on the opposite bed, facing him. "A whole lot better. Thank you."

He muted the TV and faced me, propping his head up on an elbow. "Well, well, well . . . you clean up nicely."

"Thanks," I said, looking away from his raised shirt and the tanned, lightly haired expanse of his stomach that was on full and glorious display.

"Very nicely," he mused. "I think you might be wrong about us not being the same caliber."

I didn't look away from the tacky hotel bedspread, but I could feel the weight of his scrutiny on me. And it did . . . things to me—bad things, naughty things.

He chuckled darkly, knowing precisely what I was thinking. "So, tell me about yourself, Mavis LeGrand, ice demon and Exitium Daemonium."

Shrugging, I met his lazy gaze. "There's not that much to tell. I got my MBA from the University of Utah and have—*had*—a good paying job. I was living a totally normal human life. Three hours later, here we are."

"That would make you, what, twenty-two or twenty-three, right?"

"I'm twenty-six. How old are you?"

"Older than twenty-six," he evaded.

I shook my head, smiling at him. "That means you're really old and don't want to tell me, doesn't it?"

He returned my smile. "Something like that."

"Do you plan on being this evasive all night?"

"Not at all," he said. "I plan to sleep at some point."

"Funny."

He clicked off the TV, leaving us in the dim light of the lamp between our beds. "So, what does a twenty-six-year-old college graduate do for money these days?"

"Well, this one was given an accounting job with her grandfather's firm in New York. I telecommute Monday through Friday. The job is a waste of my degree, but he didn't like me leaving the house. Sometimes, it was easier to do what he said than argue with him and his stranger-danger logic."

"Telecommute, eh? Why do I get the feeling your fake grandfather has made you somewhat of a recluse?

I frowned. "I'm not a recluse."

"You also don't have much of a life, from the sound of it."

"I have friends that I see occasionally, and I go to the library pretty frequently. I'm not a shut-in."

He coughed out, "Recluse."

I glared at him. "Well, what do you do, Cam the solitude-hating cambion?"

"I'm self-employed."

"What kind of work?" I asked.

He clenched his jaw, looking like he'd rather talk about anything else.

"Come on. It can't be that bad."

"I'm an escort," he said finally. "Women pay me to 'take them out.'"

"Take them out? Wait a minute. You steal souls and get paid for it? That's a little diabolical, isn't it?"

He waved his hand back and forth. "Yes and no."

"Yes and no, it's diabolical? Or yes, you steal souls, and no, you don't get paid for it?"

"I could deplete a human's soul over a few visits if I chose to be that big of a douchebag," he explained. "But I can't take all of it in one go. Not like my father can. And yes, I do get paid for sex, if that's what my clients want."

"Do any of your clients ever not want to have sex with you?"

He raised an eyebrow. "What do you think?"

Hugging one of the thin, but thankfully clean, bed pillows to my chest, I answered, "Honestly, I think you probably fuck a lot, Cam."

His smile was pure, unadulterated sex. "You're not wrong."

I laughed nervously. "I guess you really are your father's son."

"That I am," he said, regarding me with a look of interest.

I ignored the close examination and asked, "But you're not all incubus, right? What's your mom's half?"

"Human. Cambions are the sons and daughters of an incubus father and a human mother."

"Really? Is she in your life?"

"She died when I was six years old."

"I'm so sorry."

He waved away my concern. "It was many, many years ago, and truthfully, I was lucky to have the time I did have with her. Human women rarely survive mating with an incubus in their true form. The insemination can be violent, and the pregnancy fatal. My father was stupid to try for more offspring with her."

The angry vehemence in his voice made me flinch away from him. Noticing the movement, he said, "My father is not a topic I enjoy discussing. He is the biggest asshole I know."

"Only because you haven't spent much time with my 'grandfather,'" I grumbled.

He chuckled. "I'd say it's a demon thing, but then we'd be included in this demons-are-douchebags theory."

I unfolded my legs and scooted to the edge of the bed. "Speaking of being a demon, do you have a different form? You know, something more demon-y, or do you always look like this?"

Cam swung his legs off the bed and mimicked my position. "For a girl that was only a human yesterday, I would have thought you'd be afraid to see what a demon looks like."

"That was yesterday," I said. "Today, I'm the Exitium Daemonium, and I'm running for my life. Things have changed a bit."

He nodded. "I guess they have."

"So, let's see it. Demon out or whatever."

"Demon out?" he asked, a slight smile playing on his lips. "Sorry to disappoint, but this is my only form. If I were a true, full-blooded incubus, I could be anything you desire, male or female."

My mouth dropped open. "Anything?"

"Anything. An incubus can sense what you want and shape-shift accordingly. They'll do anything they have to, to take a soul."

"Then I'm kind of glad I don't have a soul."

"No, but you have other things an incubus, or even I, could take from you."

My breath quickened as I stared into his eyes. The shade of brown was so mesmerizing; I immediately lost myself in the flecks of dark chocolate and warm amber. "Cam, you're . . ."

"I'm what?" he asked, his gruff voice so close to my ear, I jumped.

Blinking fast, I pulled away from Cam with no memory of how I'd left my bed to join him on his.

"What just . . ." I trailed off again, staring at Cameron. His full lips looked so soft, yielding but firm at the same time. I wondered, if he kissed me, if I would feel the warm jolt I'd felt before when he touched me. I wondered if I'd feel it everywhere he touched me.

"Mavis!" he said sharply.

Coming back to myself, I shook my head to clear it. "What did you do to me?"

"I let you feel me in my natural state."

With my heart pounding, I scrambled back to my bed. "That was your natural state?"

He shot me a rueful smile. "You're still being throttled by the magic device around your heart. My charm shouldn't affect an ice demon, or any demon for that matter. Whatever that device around your heart is, it's cracked, but clearly still doing its job. The only question is if your power will be limited by the throttle permanently or if the break will slowly trickle magic into you until you're whole again."

"So, the more magic I develop, the less I'll be affected by your . . . um, charm?"

"I'm sorry, yes. You don't know how much I wish I could turn it completely off—the want, the desire. I'm holding it back as much as I can."

"I don't want you to turn it off," I said, surprising myself.

His brows lifted. "No?"

I smiled, thinking of how my body felt when I looked into his eyes. "No way. Giving myself over to your hypnotism, or whatever it is, feels decadent, delicious, like sliding into a hot bath at the end of the day. I like it. A lot."

"Yeah?" he asked.

"Yeah," I purred, matching his tone. "And that warm lick of sexual electricity you send through my body when you touch me? It's heaven."

"I like the way you describe that," he said, in a voice that could be considered foreplay. "It has a lot of my favorite words in it."

"Oh?" I asked. "Like what?"

"It has warm, and lick, and . . ."

"And what?" I asked, hanging on to every word.

"And sexual electricity."

The sound of him growling out the word *sexual* made me grab the edge of the mattress with both hands to brace myself. I swallowed hard. "Holy shit, Cam. You're really good at this seduction thing."

Cameron groaned and shifted his hips, drawing my attention downward. I gasped. He was hard—and massive. My eyes snapped back up to his.

Panic crossed his beautiful face for a split second. "Don't, Mavis."

"Don't what?" I asked, my voice barely above a whisper.

"Give in to the desire. You must resist this."

Nearly breathless with a need that was as unfamiliar as it was overwhelming, I asked, "Why?"

"Because I don't know if I can tell you no."

CHAPTER 3

I awoke to the dim orange light of the afternoon sun shining through the sheer curtains with no memory of going to bed. Worse than that, I woke up with my face smashed into a man's muscular chest. I froze, trying to get my bearings before I drew attention to myself.

A rumble of laughter sounded in my ear. "Hey there, sleepyhead. I've been wondering when you'd finally wake up."

"Cam?"

"Were you expecting it to be someone else?" he asked, amusement coloring his voice.

I peeked up at his handsome face through my crazy bed head. "No, but . . . um . . . do you mind telling me how I got here?"

"Well, let's see," he said, smoothing my hair away from my face. "If I remember correctly, I drove you here after I picked you up out of a ditch last night. You were such a dirty girl."

I rolled my eyes. "You know what I mean. Why am I half on top of your naked chest?"

He chuckled at my annoyance. "Oh, that."

"Did you . . . uh . . ."

"Did I give you the ride of your life?" he suggested, his golden-brown eyes twinkling with merriment.

"You're enjoying this far too much," I grumbled.

"I'll have you know I have a very blue pair of balls that say otherwise."

"Yeah, about that. You do realize you have a fairly large fun stick wedged against my hip, don't you?"

"As a matter of fact, I do. I also notice you haven't exactly extracted yourself from the precarious position with said 'fun stick.'"

I smiled against his smooth chest and closed my eyes, getting lost in the clean scent of his soft skin. "I'm just going to enjoy your charm for one more second. Then I'm getting up."

"Be my guest. Hell, get naked. We can continue from where we left off last night. I hear sex with me is pretty good."

"Okay," I said, springing up. "I'm done enjoying it."

Cam relaxed the arm I'd been laying on and moaned. "Oh, thank the sweet Virgin Mary. My arm has been asleep for over two hours now."

Laughing, I settled back on my knees and watched him rub the circulation back into his shoulder. Then I made the mistake of letting my gaze follow the trail of dark hair from his chest down to his stomach, and even further still, to the hard erection nearly lifting the band of his sweatpants.

"Like what you see?" he asked, catching me in the act.

"I'm not feeding your ego," I told him, shaking my head. "Your confidence is already through the roof."

A slow smile slid onto his face. "I think I'm going to like you, Mavis."

"Oh?" I asked, unable to keep the skeptical tone from my voice.

"You're all no-nonsense. It's kind of a turn-on."

"Then we're a perfect match, because you're almost all nonsense and ridiculousness. We'll probably cancel each other out."

He clutched his chest. "You wound me, demon."

"And you're a perv," I added for good measure.

"To be fair, I am a half incubus. It does kind of come with the territory."

"Yeah, about that territory . . . what happened last night? How did you end up in my bed?"

"Darling, I think you'll find we're in my bed."

I looked over at my unused double bed in horror. "What did I do?"

"You tackled me."

My eyes shot back to his. "I what?"

Cam's grin lit up his face. "You tackled me, Mavis. You tackled me, got me all hot and bothered, and then you fainted."

I stared at him, aghast. "You're making this up."

"No!" he exclaimed. "You did! One second, you had your tongue in my mouth, and the next, you were keeling over. I think after yesterday's ordeal, and the . . . what was it again?" He grinned. "Sexual electricity? I think all that excitement and you gaining some of your demon power may have overwhelmed your system."

I groaned, remembering how I'd acted while I was under his spell. I'd wanted him more than I'd ever wanted anything in my life.

"And if I hadn't passed out?" I asked. "You were just going to let me . . . um, have my way with you?"

He shook his head. "No, of course not. We didn't get to the whole consent thing before you leaped off your bed like a sexed-up cheetah."

"Noooooo," I moaned, burying my face in my hands. "I'm really sorry, Cam."

"For what? You knew I was willing."

"But still. I don't know what came over me."

He pulled my hands away from my face. "I'm a cambion, Mavis. It was me that made you do that."

"Yeah, but . . ."

"No buts," he interrupted. "You couldn't fight it if you wanted to. My gift amplifies your lust."

"So, if I weren't attracted to you, I wouldn't have . . ."

"Straddled me like you were going to ride a stallion?" he suggested, wiggling his eyebrows.

I looked skyward for help or sanity—something that would get me out of this awkward conversation.

21

"If there is anything good or just in this world, I will wake up, and this will all have been a stress-induced nightmare," I griped.

Cam settled back against the pillows, looking put out. "I think I might be offended."

"No! I didn't mean it that way!"

"Really?" he asked, sounding a little petulant.

"Really."

"I knew it," he teased. "You're hot for my fun stick."

Snaking my hand forward, I snatched the pillow out from under his head and smacked him with it. "You're going to drive me crazy!"

His grin was positively sinful. "Crazy with desire?"

"Don't flatter yourself too much. I haven't had sex in two years. I could get turned on watching a metronome tick."

"Harsh, Miss LeGrand, very harsh."

"No, it's truthful, Mr. DeSalle."

Cam studied me for a long moment before saying, "I want you to come to Colorado with me."

My brows shot up. "What's in Colorado?"

"My apartment. You'd like it there. It's freezing, just like you. Do you realize you were hovering around twenty degrees last night? It was like sleeping with an extremely hot ice block."

"Wait a minute. If you live in Colorado, what are you doing in Utah?"

"I met with a client in Provo."

"You were on your way back from a booty call?" I asked, gaping at him.

He glared at me. "No. I was on my way back from a trip to obtain a middle-aged housewife's soul in return for mind-blowing sex that she'll never forget."

I blanched. Cam's flippant charm and handsome face made it easy to forget what was underneath all that sex appeal. He wasn't an ordinary man. He was a demon, a demon that stole souls from humans. And the way he spoke so nonchalantly about it told me he didn't have any qualms about taking something so precious.

"So," he said, nudging me with his foot. "Do you want to go to Colorado with me?"

I considered him for a moment, taking in his beautiful face and seemingly sincere smile. I didn't know if I trusted him enough to go out of state with him, but honestly, what choice did I have? No one else was offering me safety and the promise of a sexual encounter, the likes of which I would never experience again. Cameron DeSalle was. And Cameron DeSalle looked to me like he'd be worth the risk.

"Mavis?" he prompted, his smile faltering when I remained quiet.

"Yes, I'll go. The farther I'm away from Leon, the better."

"Is that his name? Leon?"

"Yeah, Leon LeGrand."

He nodded. "You'll be safe from him in Havenwood Falls, Mavis. I promise."

"Safe sounds outstanding, Cam. Thank you."

"It's the least I can do. Besides, I'm looking forward to spending more time with you. You've put a little excitement into an old demon's very mundane life."

"How old?" I asked, my interest piqued.

"I was born in nineteen sixteen."

I did a little quick math in my head. "Wow. You are old."

"And you were raised by an evil demon, so I'll ignore your rudeness."

"Sorry. I wasn't expecting you to be quite that . . . experienced."

He huffed. "That's better."

"Uh-oh. Is someone sensitive about his age?"

"No, but someone is going to be riding in the truck bed to Colorado if she keeps it up."

"Duly noted," I said, laughing at his sour expression. "The teasing stops now."

Relaxing back into the pillows, he sighed in exaggerated relief. "Good. Because I can dish it out, but I can't take it."

CHAPTER 4

$\mathcal{C}$am pulled into a random diner's parking lot a few hours after we left the hotel. I grinned at him and jumped out of the truck with exuberance.

"A diner!" I squealed.

"Wait until I put the truck in park," he yelled, jumping out after me.

"I've never been anywhere like this before," I explained happily. "It looks just like the diners do on TV."

"And how's that?"

"You know, small and clean with red leather booths and fifties décor. That kind of thing."

"Well, then, I'm glad I picked the only restaurant open this time of night," he said, winking as he opened the door for me.

"Sit anywhere you like," a waitress called out to us. "What can I get you two to drink?"

"I'll have coffee," Cam said, giving her a friendly grin that made her nearly drop the plate she was delivering to the single patron sitting at the bar. "Black, no sugar, please."

"And for your sister?" she asked, apparently dazed by Cam's siren song.

"A soda is fine," I muttered, feeling irrationally irritated with the mile-long-legged curvy blonde that was practically having eye foreplay with my favorite new demon friend.

Trying to hide his bemused smile, Cam told the waitress, "My wife will have a Coke," and led me to the back booth.

The blonde's come-hither smile fell, but she recovered fairly quickly for the sake of her tip. "Coming right up."

"I think you have a fan," I teased, once we were seated.

"She can't help herself, Mavis. I'm irresistible."

"And so modest, too," I complained, picking up a menu.

"Jealous, little ice demon?"

I ignored the bait in favor of scanning the extensive menu. "Oh, look! They have biscuits! I've always wanted to try a biscuit."

Cam stared at me. "Are you telling me you've never been to a diner and you've never had a biscuit? Never . . . in twenty-six years?"

"I'm telling you we had a personal chef that prepared all our meals, none of which included biscuits. My grandfather would never eat something so common. He has his tastes and ways and isn't a huge fan of people. I guess that makes more sense now that I know he's a demon."

"Tell me more about this snobby, reclusive demon with the colorful language. How dangerous is he? Should I be calling for backup?"

"Do you have backup?"

"No, but I could probably scrounge together a small crew of supernatural misfits if I need to."

"That's good to know. Because my grandfather is something of a monster, from what I read in his journal."

"Here's your coffee, handsome," the waitress purred as she made her way to our table and leaned across Cameron to set down the white ceramic mug on his other side. She took her time straightening before she lightly slammed my soda on the table next to me. "And your wife's Coke," she said, nearly sneering at me.

When she sashayed back behind the counter to fill salt shakers, I asked, "You don't think she poisoned me, do you?" and sniffed the contents of the plastic tumbler.

He chuckled. "No, I watched her fill the cup. Know what you want?"

"Right now? Personal safety. On so, so many levels."

"And?" he pressed.

I shrugged. "World peace?"

Cam narrowed his eyes. "From the menu, smarty-pants."

"Oh," I said, my eyes wide and innocent. "The Biscuit Supreme, please."

"Thank you," he said, taking my menu with exaggerated exasperation.

He motioned to the waitress, who snapped to attention the moment she saw his hand. "What'll you have, handsome?"

"We'll have the Apple Walnut French Toast and Biscuit Supreme, please."

She beamed at Cam like he'd asked for her hand in marriage instead of our breakfast. "Coming right up."

"Thank you, Breanne," he said, making a show of reading the nametag on her chest while handing her our menus.

She giggled and straightened her top, pushing her breasts closer to Cam's face. "You're welcome, lover."

Finally fed up with her blatant flirting, I cleared my throat loudly.

Breanne shot a nasty look my way for interrupting whatever she thought she had going on with Cam, but the action had the desired effect. She stormed away to turn in the order, shooting daggers my way every few seconds.

"Am I going to have to break up a cat fight between you two?" Cam asked, looking more than pleased with himself.

"I'm not going to say it's off the table," I seethed.

"Mavis, you're not my real wife. Don't worry about the waitress."

I huffed in frustration. "It's the principle of the thing, Cam. She's disrespecting me." I glared over my shoulder at the waitress. "And I may just have to kick her ass for it."

He sat back and studied me thoughtfully with his arms crossed. "I think I enjoy seeing you riled up. You're all demonic claws and teeth underneath that librarian spinster façade. It's sexy."

"Librarian spinster?" I spat. "Am I going to have to kick your ass, too?"

Cam raised his hands defensively. "Hey, now. I was paying you a compliment."

"Some compliment," I muttered.

He smirked. "Do you want a better one, wifey?"

I squinted at him, knowing he was up to something but decided to indulge him anyway. "You know what, hubby? I think I might."

Cam took a sip of his coffee and moved the cup to the far side of the table so that he could lean toward me.

I met him halfway. "Well?"

"There's nothing about you I couldn't compliment. You're smart and pretty, and you've got these perfect hand-sized breasts and this luscious ass that makes me want to—"

"That'll do," I said, interrupting him.

"But I'm not done."

"Oh, you're done," I assured him.

He flashed a panty-dropping smile at me and stage-whispered, "I like how hard you make me."

"Shh!" I hissed.

"What?" he said, in a much louder voice. "I can't tell the whole room how much I want my sexy, beautiful wife? Why not? It's not a lie." He grinned at the customer at the bar and the waitress, who had just come out of the kitchen with our plates. "I'd be tempted to get her naked right here on this table if it wasn't illegal."

The waitress reacted to this information by stomping her way to our table to drop off our food, then fuming all the way back to the kitchen. The customer just laughed and asked, "Newlyweds?"

Cam grinned. "Yes, sir. We met in Vegas, and I just knew she would change my life. I'm taking her home to North Dakota with me."

"Well, I wish you both the best," the old man said, getting up and throwing a twenty-dollar bill on the counter. "Take care, now."

"Thanks," we said in unison.

When I heard the tinkle of the doorbell and knew we were alone, I turned on Cam. "What are you doing?"

Switching our plates, he cut a maple-syrup-drenched bite of French toast and chewed it before he answered. "Trying to make you smile. I like it when you smile. The frowning thing, not so much."

"You don't think that way was a bit extreme?"

"It had a dual purpose."

"And what could that possibly be?"

"It's so people remember us as a newlywed couple on their way from Las Vegas to North Dakota. Even if you are recognized, they'll be looking for you a few states away."

I stared at him. "You are something else, Cameron DeSalle."

"I meant what I said. I do think you're smart and pretty, and I do think you're going to change my life."

"Really?"

"Really," he assured me.

I sighed. "Well, now I'm disappointed that you didn't mention my perfect, hand-sized breasts and luscious—"

"That'll do," he said, mocking my earlier words.

"But I'm not done."

"Oh, you're done," he said, grinning at me. "Eat your biscuit, little demon."

WITH FULL STOMACHS, Cam and I piled back into the truck and set out for Colorado. I couldn't wait to get there. Going somewhere I would never have to worry about Leon again sounded like heaven. I just hoped living with me wouldn't be hell for Cam. With his lifestyle, I was bound to get in his way.

"What are you thinking about?" Cam asked.

"About the future."

"I think we'd better focus on the short term. We have to get you somewhere safe before we start worrying about the future."

Dejected, I sat back in my seat. "I feel so helpless, Cam."

"Which is why I'm helping you."

"Distracting me is more like it."

"That, too," he agreed. "As I said, I like it when you smile."

"Is it because you like to see me happy or because you want to make sure I don't start killing demons with some ridiculous power I know nothing about?"

He laughed. "When you put it that way, I'd have to say both."

I groaned. "What am I going to do?"

"Turn on the heat? You've got it freezing in here."

"Sorry," I said, trying to stop whatever I was doing.

"Close your eyes, Mavis. I'll help you."

I obeyed. "Now what?"

"Calm yourself. Center yourself. All those worries you have, just let them drift away. Now I want you to take a breath in through your nose for four seconds. After that, hold that breath for seven seconds. Then I want you to slowly blow it out your mouth for eight seconds and tell me how you feel."

I opened my eyes. "Do what now?"

"Inhale through your nose for four seconds, hold it for seven, and let it go for eight seconds. Here, I'll do it with you."

We both took in a slow breath as Cam counted to four with his fingers, then held it for seven seconds. Closing my eyes, I slowly let go of my breath for the eight seconds and let my head roll to the side.

Smiling over at him, I asked, "Where did you learn that?"

"One of my clients suffers from anxiety attacks after sex sometimes. I help her calm down before I leave."

"That's sweet of you."

He shrugged. "I don't mind. She's paying me a small fortune to steal her soul. It's the least I can do."

"Do you like the sex you have with your clients, or is it like any other job after a while?"

"Honestly, I can't imagine anyone enjoying prostitution."

"Then why do you do it?"

"Because I don't want to hurt innocent women. The women I escort aren't faithful. I make sure of it. If I have to collect souls from women, I want to take them from those who might be going south already."

"Do all cambions and incubuses have your stellar moral fiber?"

"Not any that I've ever met. They only have one goal—collecting souls."

"What makes you so different?"

He hesitated before answering. "When I was a kid, I had every possibility in front of me. I could be or do anything. Then my mom died, and I was left to be raised by an incubus. This is not the life my mother would have wanted for me, Mavis. Every demon knows right from wrong. It's what you do with that knowledge that matters."

I stayed silent, just processing for a moment. "Do you have to do this? Is it mandatory for your kind?"

"My father told me, in no uncertain terms, that if I do not collect souls for him, he will take the soul my mother gave me himself."

I gritted my teeth. "He would do that to his child?"

"He would do that to his one and only child," he assured me. "I'm nothing but an embarrassment to him. He has no use for a son who doesn't want to hurt humans and won't obey his every command. He says my mother spoiled me by not teaching me to think and act like a demon."

"That makes no sense. How would she even know how to do that? She was human."

"Yes, and so am I, and apparently, that is unforgivable in his eyes."

"But he was the one who . . . uh . . . mated with her, right? It's not like he didn't know you'd be half human."

"Of course he knew. There is no other choice for us. Incubuses can't procreate naturally. They don't have souls. The only way to impregnate a human is to acquire sperm from a succubus's victim and transfer it to the host while in their true form."

I wrinkled my nose. "Ew."

"Yeah," he agreed.

"Being a demon isn't all it's cracked up to be, is it?" I asked.

He chuckled and shook his head. "I don't think anyone hears 'demon' and thinks it's the greatest thing ever."

"No, but damn, Cam. You fuck people pretty much against your will, and I was born to be some ice-loving demon killer. What the shit is that? There's got to be something good about it."

"You forget that you're immortal."

"Oh, yeah. Great. We can have these horrible lives for an eternity."

Cam came to a stop at a red light and met my eyes. "Even the most horrible life has its good moments, Mavis."

CHAPTER 5

*C*am and I talked almost the entire drive to Havenwood Falls. I
learned that he loved horror movies (the bloodier, the better),
hiking, and strawberry rhubarb pie. He discovered that I hated all
those things and that I didn't appreciate his critique of my favorite
movies and books. But to be fair, there are only so many times a
demoness can hear the word *overrated* before she snaps.

Our bickering about Colin Firth's acting abilities aside, it was nice
to get to know more about Cam. From what we'd discussed, I could
tell he was planning to keep me around for a while. Knowing his likes
and dislikes would make it easier for me to keep my new roommate
happy and be less of a nuisance to him. Plus, underneath all that sexy
brooding, he was an interesting demon—an opinionated, sex-driven
trickster of a demon, but an interesting demon, nonetheless.

On the last stretch of our trip, Cam was quiet, so I kept myself
entertained by watching the scenery fly by the window. The trees were
beautiful here, majestic and magical in the bright moonlight. I took a
deep breath, feeling a liberating sort of freedom flow through me. I
was almost to safety.

Cam gestured up ahead. "We're nearly there."

Looking to where he pointed, I saw the black metal-and-stone sign
welcoming us to Havenwood Falls.

"What's it like?" I asked excitedly.

He shrugged. "It's Havenwood Falls. It's home."

I laughed. "Care to elaborate on that?"

He sighed. "I might as well. You'll have to know soon enough."

"Know what?"

"Well, first, there are supernatural beings of every sort there."

I stared at him, mouth agape.

He smiled at my reaction. "Mavis, Havenwood Falls is not like other towns. It has safeguards in place that make it nearly impossible to find. You won't even find it on Google Maps. That alone makes it a refuge for supernatural creatures and humans alike. There's nowhere in the world you could be more protected than here."

"How is it protected? Dragons?"

"By magic and strict rules. The dragons pretty much keep to themselves."

I shook my head, dumbfounded by what I was hearing. "How strict are the rules?"

"They're nothing crazy. It's basically just don't be a dick and don't reveal yourself to the humans."

"Does that ever happen?"

"Very, very rarely. All supernaturals, including demons, whether visitors or residents, have to register with the Court of the Sun and the Moon. They'll give you a tattoo that will hide your true nature from the rest of the population."

"A tattoo?" I screeched. "No way. I'm not getting a tattoo."

"If you intend on staying, you will. It's required. You can pick whatever you want, and it can even be invisible. It's not a big deal. Plus, we don't know what you'll look like if your power decides to make an appearance. The tattoo will keep the humans from seeing what you look like in your demon form."

I paled in shock. "W-what do you mean?"

"Mavis, ice demons differ from almost all of the other demons. They do not naturally look human unless you have one as a parent. The beautiful woman in front of me is some sort of glamour, no doubt included in that throttle of yours."

I stared at him in horror. "What?"

"Don't tell me you didn't already think of this. You asked me to see my true form last night."

"But I didn't think of it," I told him. "I can't believe I didn't, but I didn't. Is it terrible?"

"Beauty is in the eye of the beholder, of course, but I will tell you that the few ice demons I've seen look pretty similar to each other. They have very, very pale skin, white-blond hair, and silver eyes. The males have these huge intimidating horns and large patches of ice crystals spread out over their body. The females have smaller, daintier horns and tiny patches of ice along their temples and shoulders."

I shuddered. "That sounds hideous."

"Honestly, the females are pretty hot as far as demons go. You'll still look the same, just with paler features. And those horns really are adorable."

"Is that supposed to reassure me?"

"Not in the slightest. If anything, it's supposed to let you know I'm game for sex with you no matter what you look like."

I shook my head. "You're incorrigible."

"And you're home," he said, as the streetlamp-lit town appeared before us.

"Wow," I exclaimed, surprised at how charming and picturesque the town was, even from here. "It's beautiful."

"It's one of my favorite sights on the planet."

"It's easy to see why," I said, smiling at the proud expression on his face.

Cam drove slowly in the darkness, allowing me to take in everything I could. Soon after entering the town, I saw the grand entrance of Creekwood Estates and Country Club, Havenwood Falls High School, and a shopping center, Miller's Plaza. All the businesses and food shops in the plaza looked closed for the night, but I could imagine them lively and full of people during the day.

I grinned at Cam. "We're so far into the mountains, I thought it would be a one-horse town, but this is amazing!"

He returned my excited smile. "I am rather fond of it."

"How long have you lived here?"

"Since I was very small. There are some types of demons that will kill a cambion if they can get close enough. Havenwood Falls was the safest place for us."

My jaw dropped. "Well, that's not terrifying or anything. I'm glad your parents put you somewhere safe."

"Trust me. My father only wanted to protect his investment. Wouldn't you, if you got credit with the bigwigs downstairs for every piece of soul I steal?"

"And the town is okay with you stealing souls? That doesn't fall under the don't-be-a-dick edict?"

"The Court has never approved of stealing souls, which you would've seen firsthand had you shown up a few months ago when some of the mammon demons got banished."

"Then why do they let you do it?" I asked.

"Because my case is different than theirs. I don't do it because I want to hurt humans; I do it because my soul literally depends on me keeping my father happy, so they're a little sympathetic to my plight. Not to mention, I'm a long-time resident who has never caused one iota of trouble. The only caveat they've given me is that I'm not allowed to sleep with anyone in the town limits."

I shook my head in disgust. "Your father is a piece of work. He really doesn't have any redeeming qualities, does he?"

"Not even one," he answered darkly. "Which is the reason he's only allowed to visit Havenwood Falls every few weeks. And really, that's only because I've lobbied the Court on his behalf and assured them that I can keep him on the straight and narrow."

"Why would you do that for him, after everything he's done to you?"

"Because the alternative is a cranky, pissed off demon who will make my life a nightmare," he said simply. "It's true what they say about keeping your enemies closer, you know."

"Demons," I said, sighing and clucking my tongue.

Cam laughed and pulled into a driveway, parking next to a building labeled *C*. He turned off the engine and aimed a mischievous smile at me. "Welcome to Havenwood Village."

I smiled back, but couldn't seem to get myself to move from the warmth of the truck.

"Is it weird that I'm suddenly super nervous to see your apartment?" I asked.

He drew a halo around his head with a finger. "I promise to keep my hands to myself."

"I'll believe that when I see it," I told him, reaching for my door.

He stopped me with a gentle hand on my arm. "I'm serious. Until you can resist my charm, I don't think that it's a good idea for us to have sex. I wouldn't feel right about it."

"I don't think it's a good idea for us to have sex under any circumstances, Cam, but that doesn't keep me from wanting it," I told him.

His eyes roamed from my face to my body, then he sighed. "Me neither, Mavis. Me neither."

"So we're agreed on no sex until my magic shows up all the way?"

He nodded.

"What if it never does?"

He shrugged and sat back in his seat. "I reserve the right to make addendums after an appropriate amount of time."

"Then I accept your terms," I told him, offering a handshake. "Any more ground rules?"

He accepted my hand but didn't shake it. He only held it in both of his own, examining the lines on my palm for who knew what. "Just the usual. No smoking, no pets, no illicit drugs, and no demon-killing inside the town limits. The Court will give you the freedom to figure this out on your own, but one big slipup, and they'll swoop in on us like a SWAT team."

"Anything else?" I asked, surprised by the sensual sound of my voice.

He grinned and let go of my hand. "Try not to walk around naked in front of me."

"Trust me. You have nothing to worry about there. You're the one with the positive body image, remember?"

Cam scoffed. "Of course it's positive. Have you seen my body?"

I rolled my eyes. "As usual, your modesty astounds me."

"You'd think you'd have lowered your expectations by now," he said, opening the door.

MY FIRST IMPRESSION of Cam's apartment was that it was sparkling clean, but it had the sparsely decorated, sad look of a place that was only used for a place to sleep. It made me wonder how often Cam went out of town on his "business trips."

"Your bedroom is at the end of the hall on the right," Cam said, directing me to the hallway off the right of the living room. "Your bathroom is on the left."

I peered down the darkened hallway. "Where's your room?"

He turned in the opposite direction and pointed to an identical setup at the other end of the apartment. "Right down there. The kitchen and laundry are through the doorway before the hallway."

"Okay," I said, fidgeting with a loose thread on the hem of my shirt. I couldn't think of anything to say now that we were here and alone.

"It's awkward now, right?" he asked.

I laughed. "So awkward. But we'll figure it out."

He smiled that devastatingly handsome smile of his and nodded. "That we will. I still want to get in your pants. I'm willing to play nice as long as it takes."

"You are a terrible demon," I said, shaking my head.

"I know. It's both a blessing and a curse." He grinned and opened my bedroom door. Flipping on the light switch, he said, "The sheets should be relatively fresh, and there are extra blankets in your closet if you get cold. It can get a little chilly at night."

"I doubt I'll have to worry about that," I said, rolling my eyes. "Cold is sort of my thing."

"Well, it's not mine. I sleep in the nude. I want to keep my shrinkage to a minimum."

I snorted. "Understood. I'll try my best to keep myself at room temperature."

"See that you do," he said, smiling down at me. "So, see you in the morning?"

"I'll see you then. If you have trouble recognizing me, I'll be the burden you picked up in Utah."

"You're not a burden, Mavis. I told you I'd help you, and I will. I keep my promises."

"I know," I said, letting out a heavy sigh. "I just feel like I'm going to get in your way."

"You won't," he assured me. Then he grinned mischievously and poked my shoulder with a finger. "And if you do, I'll just give you a little shove."

"As long as you realize that I'll shove you back," I retorted, putting both palms on his rock-hard chest and giving him a little push.

He slid his fingers into the hair at my temples and pressed a soft, lingering kiss to my forehead.

"Sleep well, Mavis." His voice was low and husky, and his brow was creased with concentration as if he was struggling to keep his actions chaste.

I slid my palms down to the waistband of his jeans, never taking my eyes off his. "Sweet dreams, Cam."

"You move your hands any lower, and they're going to be sex dreams instead of sweet dreams," he warned, backing me up against the wall.

"You mean, like this?" I asked, tracing the hard outline of his erection through the denim.

Cam hissed and spoke with clenched teeth. "What about our agreement, Mavis?"

I popped the button on his jeans. "Fuck the agreement."

His eyes flared with desire. "Tempting, but how about I fuck you instead?" he asked, sending shockwave after shockwave of power through me when he moved his hands to cup my ass.

Instead of answering, I kept my gaze locked on his, slowly and deliberately lowering his zipper.

"Mavis," he growled, his tone pleading.

"Shh," I whispered, taking his hard length into my palms and stroking him from base to tip.

"Fuck, Mavis!" he shouted, bucking in my hands.

"I think that's what we're doing," I teased.

He groaned with restrained pleasure and pulled away, gasping for air. "My bedroom, little demon. Now."

Without a word, I walked away, shedding my clothes as I went.

Cam trailed slowly behind me, taking in my strip show in silence. When he reached me, he looked at me from head to toe, hunger darkening his brown eyes to nearly black. His erection was as hard as a rock as he pulled off his shirt and pushed his jeans down his muscular thighs.

"I'll try to be as gentle as I can," he said, though his face told me the exact opposite.

"Don't you dare," I told him bravely. "I want all of you."

"Don't forget you said that," he said, his smile downright devious as he joined me on the bed and tugged me up to his body.

I went willingly. I was aching to touch him, to taste him, but as much as I desired him, I was hesitant to make the first move. I wanted this to be perfect. Cam wasn't some frat boy in the back of a Camaro. He was a professional.

Cam raised his brows. "Are you okay?"

I chuckled. "You're not going to believe this, but I'm a little nervous."

He smiled. "Good."

"Why is that good?" I asked.

He threaded his fingers in my hair, his lips so close to mine, I could practically taste him. "You know why."

And when Cam pressed his lips against mine, I did know why. It was in the way he laid out his need for me in his kiss, the way he seemed desperate to relay what he couldn't say in words. He didn't want this to be another job for him. He wanted something real.

And so did I. As much as I enjoyed the way his charm made me feel, it didn't compare with the genuine lust and affection I felt for him when he touched me like he was doing now.

Cam lifted his head to gauge my reaction, then retook my mouth, licking it open to deepen the kiss.

I groaned and sagged against him. "Please," I whispered against his lips.

Nodding slightly, he kissed me again, urgently this time. Then he settled on his knees between my legs.

I arched against his heavy erection. "Please, Cameron."

Without preamble, he positioned himself at my core and started to push inside slowly. His eyes were closed, and his teeth gritted in concentration.

I whimpered at the pleasured pain.

He stilled, his eyes searching my face. "Mavis?"

"Don't stop," I panted. "I want you."

Resigned, Cam bent his head to take my mouth, swallowing my cries until he was finally fully seated within me. Then, with aching slowness, he withdrew and pushed back in, making me moan into his mouth.

"Please," I begged, wanting him to fuck me until I couldn't think anymore.

Groaning, he hitched up my legs and pumped hard and fast, eliciting a pleasured scream from me as the delicious pressure I craved ratcheted up.

I clung to his shoulders, letting him set the furious pace that was bringing me closer and closer to orgasm. "Harder!" I cried out.

Cam obliged, moving into me so fast and hard, he lifted me off the mattress with every thrust. "Come for me, Mavis."

As soon as the words came from his lips, I had no choice. I seized up all at once, screaming out his name.

He followed right after, roaring as he spilled deep inside of me.

I laughed as he rested his forehead against mine then sighed. "Well, that was long overdue . . . for both of us."

He grinned. "I was honestly worried about waking up stuck to the bed in the morning."

"That is way hotter than it should be," I told him.

"You're way hotter than you should be," he shot back.

I rolled my hips. "Is that why you're still hard?"

He groaned. "It's not like I have a lot of choice in the matter. Mavis, you were so hot and wet for me, I can't help but want more of you."

"Were?" I asked wickedly. "Cam, if you haven't noticed, I'm still hot and wet for you."

"Fancy a ride, then?" he asked, rolling us over so that I was on top of him.

"I thought you'd never ask," I said, starting a cadence that had him digging his fingers into my hips and meeting my thrusts.

He chuckled. "Believe me. It hasn't been easy."

I leaned down and nipped at his lips. "Well, if I would've known it would be this good, I might've given in the night we met."

"So you're saying you like?"

I offered him a sultry smile. "Oh, I like a lot."

"What else do you like?"

"I like the feel of you inside of me. I like that look of restraint on your face. I think it's hot as fuck that you're holding back what you want to do to me."

His brows lifted in surprise. "What do you think I want to do?"

"I don't think," I purred. "I know. You want to dominate me, make me beg for your cock, fuck me so hard and good, it makes me wet every time I think about your dick."

His eyes were as black as coal as he asked, "And if I said that was all true? How would you feel about that?"

"If I didn't want that, I wouldn't be here right now, Cam. You're half incubus. I know what that entails."

"And if I say I want more than that from you?"

"I'll give it to you. I'll give you anything you want. I want you to ruin me for every other demon."

"Anything I want?"

"Name it."

"I want you to get a particular tattoo tomorrow, one that marks you as being under my protection."

"Done. Anything else?"

"Yes," he said, slipping his hand between us. "I want you to come, because I'm not going to last much longer."

CHAPTER 6

*C*am was still sleeping when I finally slipped out from under his arm and padded to the bathroom the next afternoon. I had been loath to do it. I loved being tangled up with him in our cozy little nest of sheets and blankets. It had been so warm and comfortable, and his dick had been so very accessible.

I shook my head and laughed to myself. The night before had been . . . I didn't think there were words for what the night before had been. Cameron was a fantastic lover. His dedication to pleasing me had been something to behold.

And I hoped to behold it at least ten more times before the day was over.

The only thing I was unsure about was what the sex had meant to Cam. It was true that he was half incubus, so it was possible that he just wanted to fuck, but somehow, what we'd done didn't feel like casual sex. What I was starting to feel for him didn't feel casual at all. It felt right. I just hoped he felt the same for me.

Ridiculously giddy at the thought of rejoining Cam and his nakedness, I closed the bathroom door and found the light switch. And then I screamed bloody murder.

Cam burst through the door seconds later. His eyes were wild with worry. "Mavis! What is it?"

Holding up a shaky finger, I pointed to myself in the mirror, but I couldn't seem to make words come out of my mouth.

"Oh, that." He gave me a warm smile. "You're beautiful."

I glared at him. "I'm hideous, Cam!"

"You're an ice demon. Ice demons aren't hideous."

"What the fuck is going on in here?" asked a feminine voice from outside the bathroom.

Cam and I both jerked our gazes to the owner of the voice. She was a tall, pretty woman with long brown hair and laughing chocolate-colored eyes. And I'd never seen her before in my life.

"Hi. I'm Penelope," she said, her smile fading as she looked down. "Wow. You guys are really super naked."

I looked over to Cam, who was holding a hand towel over his crotch and trying not to laugh. He didn't seem to be surprised by the strange woman in his apartment or worried that she was witnessing his demon friend have a nervous breakdown.

"Mavis," he said, trying to regain his composure. "This is my neighbor from next door, Penelope Osbourne. Penelope, this is my girlfriend, Mavis. She just moved in last night."

"I get the feeling that a lot of things happened last night," she said, motioning to me and my brand spanking new demon face.

I threw my hands up. "Thank you! Can we get back to the crisis at hand? Look at me!" I cried, pointing at the demon with the unnaturally pale face and hair in the mirror. "Wait! Did you say I was your girlfriend?"

Cam chuckled at my one-eighty and wrapped his free arm around my waist. "Yes, I said girlfriend. And I am looking at you, darling. Trust me. If this towel weren't here, I would show you just how much I like the view."

"Gross," Penelope groaned dramatically. "I think I just threw up in my mouth."

"And I think I just heard the washer stop," Cam told her pointedly.

"Subtle, Cam," she said, going back the way she'd come. "Very subtle."

I grabbed a towel to wrap around myself and ran after her. "Wait! Are you a demon, too?"

Penelope laughed. "Nope, just an ordinary human."

"But you're so calm about . . ." I gestured to everything that was going on in the bathroom. "All of this."

She shrugged. "I've known Cam is a demon since I was in high school. The walls are thin, and I'm super nosy. I know plenty of things most of the humans here are oblivious to."

"But how are you not affected by his charm? I thought all humans were affected."

"I told you that the local monsters get a tattoo," Cam reminded me. "This is a prime example of why."

"It's a good thing it works, too," Penelope said, humor coloring her voice. "Otherwise, I'd be humping his leg or something."

My jaw dropped. Did Cam have that kind of power over humans?

"She's just kidding," Cam said, rolling his eyes.

Penelope shook her head from the doorway and mouthed, "No, I'm not," behind his back.

"This day took a bizarre turn," I said, suddenly too exhausted to stand.

Cam led me back to the bedroom and sat me down on the foot of the bed. "You need to calm down. You'll go back to normal soon."

I sighed in relief. "Good."

Penelope looked to Cam in confusion. "But isn't this her natural state?"

Cam shot her a warning look.

"Right," she said, taking the hint. "You know, I think you're right. The washer is done. I'll just put my stuff in the dryer and see myself out. It was nice meeting you, Mavis."

"You, too, Penelope," I said. Then I turned on Cam. "Is she right?"

He cringed under my stare. "Technically, yes. She's right. But as I said, you can go back to the Mavis you've known your entire life if you just calm down. Do the breathing exercise I taught you."

"I can't be like this forever," I whined, falling back onto the bed.

"You can, and more importantly, you will." He smiled as he

absentmindedly stroked my ankle. "You're so beautiful like this. You don't even realize how much."

"I look like a creature of Hell."

"You are a creature of Hell. We both are. Now put your big-girl panties on and deal with it."

I sighed. "I don't even know where my panties are."

Cam stifled a smile and held out a hand to me. "Come here."

"Why? Where are we going?" I asked, warily putting my hand into his.

He opened the closet door to show me a full-length mirror hung inside. "I want to show you something."

"What?" I asked, barely able to look at what I'd become.

"Do you know what I see when I look at you?"

"A demon?"

"A beautiful demon," he corrected. "Everything about the way you look makes my cock hard . . . everything." He ran his palms down my shoulders. "Your luminescent skin, the otherworldly look to your eyes and hair, those ridiculously adorable horns . . . all of it makes me want to fuck you."

"Cam . . ."

He cut me off with a finger to my lips. "No arguments, Mavis. And no more degrading yourself. You were stunning before, and you still are. Maybe even more so."

"But . . ."

"Don't make me spank you, little miss demoness," he whispered in my ear. "Because I will."

My brows shot up as I felt him press his hardness into the small of my back. "Are you threatening me, Mr. DeSalle?"

"That depends on you," he told me, nuzzling my neck.

I relaxed against his bare chest and tilted my head to the side to give him better access. "Oh?"

"Yeah," he said, loosening the towel from my breasts and letting it fall to the floor. "It depends on whether you'll take a damn compliment or if you'll continue to be stubborn."

"I'm a little tempted to be stubborn when you make it sound all sexy like that."

He barked out a laugh. "And I'm the incorrigible one?"

I scoffed. "Without a doubt."

"Not even one?" he asked.

Cam's dubious face made me laugh. "Stop trying to cheer me up and commiserate with me."

"Would but I could," he said. "I can't have sympathy for you if I don't think there's anything wrong."

"I bet your tune will change once you have to have sex with me like this."

He smiled at me in the mirror and kissed my neck. "I had sex with you like this for hours last night."

I snaked my hand behind me and smacked what I could reach, which turned out to be his naked hip. "Why didn't you tell me?"

"Because I knew you'd freak out, and I didn't want it to ruin our first night together. Plus, it was sexy as fuck seeing you like this for the first time." He lifted a finger to one of my horns and ran it from the tip, down my cheek, into my cleavage, and finally across my waist, before plunging into my heated flesh. "You don't know how beautiful you were last night."

I moaned loudly, my hips bucking forward against his hand, chasing his hard and fast rhythm.

Cam's smile was wicked as he watched me writhe around his talented fingers. "Open your eyes. I want you to see what I do when you come."

I did as he asked, but I couldn't look at myself, not when I could see Cam as he was right now. His face was wild, animalistic in its intensity. He was barely in control.

"I want you inside me," I said, locking eyes with him.

Without hesitation, Cam grabbed me by the waist and lifted me onto his rigid sex. Instinctively, I wrapped my legs around his thighs and fell forward, bracing my hands on either side of the mirror. He slid his hands under my knees to support my weight and groaned as he watched my breasts bounce with every pump of his cock between my legs.

"Come, Mavis," he demanded.

I was helpless to disobey, screaming out my climax so loud, I thought I might shatter the mirror. Cam followed right after with a sharp yell and sank to his knees, taking me down with him.

When we'd calmed down, and we were no longer breathing like we'd run a marathon, I started laughing and continued to laugh until big fat tears were leaking down my cheeks.

Cam looked at me like he was concerned for my sanity. "What's so funny?"

Wiping tears from my eyes, I said, "All this time, and I didn't even notice."

"Notice what?"

"The sexual electricity, it's gone."

He laughed and stood to help me to my feet. "You didn't notice?"

I slid my arms around his waist and kissed his chest, careful not to poke him with my horns. "I don't notice a lot of things when you have your cock in me," I said. "It's very distracting."

"A good distraction?" he asked, tugging me forward to kiss my lips.

I grinned and pecked him on the lips. "The best kind of distraction."

HOURS LATER, when we finally made it out of the bedroom to shower and rejoin civilization, Cam answered the doorbell and let in a pretty woman with long, light brown hair, brown eyes, and a sparkling diamond stud in her nose, to tattoo my upper arm. Adelaide Beaumont, or Addie for short, was a witch and a member of what Cam called the Luna Coven, and she was in a big hurry, which was evident by the way she went to work after only a cursory introduction. I tried not to watch while she did her work, concentrating on the soft sound of her many bracelets and bangles to distract myself. When she'd finished, she nodded at the strange symbol she'd drawn at Cam's direction, packed her things, and asked Cam to walk her outside. With a wave and a grin, she said goodbye to me and was gone as quickly as she'd come.

After a minute or so, Cam returned, looking resolute. I watched him close the door, then said, "Well, that was anticlimactic."

He gave me an indulgent smile. "I told you it was no big deal, didn't I?"

"You did," I said, gingerly touching my arm. I was surprised there was no pain or tenderness. "But you know, it was needles, so . . ."

He laughed. "So, how about dinner? What are you thinking?"

"Pizza?" I suggested.

"Sounds good. Napoli's has the best pizza this side of the Mississippi. You just wait. You'll love it. Do you know what kind you want to order?"

I squinted at him. He didn't realize it, but this was a pivotal moment in our budding relationship. His pizza choice might be the deal breaker I'd been anticipating since he tossed out the girlfriend card.

"What?" he asked, looking at my skeptical face with nervousness.

"What kind of pizza do you like?"

"Anything. As long as it doesn't have pineapple on it."

I blew out a breath. "Oh, thank God! If you would've been one of those awful pineapple lovers, I would have had to find some other demon to take me to his hometown and make me his love slave."

He rolled his eyes as he grabbed his phone, but I could tell he was amused. "So, pepperoni is good?"

"More than good, but be warned. If you pick the toppings, I get to pick the movie."

Cam eyed me suspiciously. "I think it might be better if you pick the pizza."

"Why?"

"Librarian spinster," he said, waving an arm in my direction.

"And what is that supposed to mean?"

"It means that my TV has a No Jane feature. No Jane Austen. No Jane Eyre."

"Who said I even watch those movies?"

"Uh, you did, on the car ride here, remember?"

I grinned. "Oh, yeah."

"So?"

"Half cheese, half pepperoni."

"Perfect. Just don't ask me for any of my side."

I plopped down on his cushy beige couch and sighed petulantly. "Aren't you supposed to be wooing me?"

"Do you need wooing?" he asked, kneeling in front of me with a smirk that made him look like a cat that had eaten several canaries.

"Maybe."

"Then let me get right on that," he growled, seconds before the doorbell rang.

Cam jumped to his feet. "Fuck."

Alarmed, I sat up straight. "What? What's happening?"

He glowered at the door. "It's my father."

CHAPTER 7

The moment I saw Severin DeSalle, I knew I would hate him. A tall dark-haired and dark-eyed male, he was dressed in a black suit that hugged his muscled frame beautifully, but his face was snarled in a sneer that spoke volumes of his disdain for his only spawn.

"Father," Cameron said in greeting, nodding his head in respect.

Instead of responding, the demon ignored him and walked across the room to the couch I sat on. His eyes traveled the length of my body before he bestowed me with a smile that promised sexual delights the likes of which I'd never experienced. "Cameron, introduce me to your lady friend. She is positively delicious."

I cringed inwardly but managed to slap a friendly smile on my face and ask, "Was that a compliment, Mr. DeSalle, or do you want to eat me for dessert?"

His dazzling smile widened. "As tempting as eating you would be, it was only meant as a compliment, Miss . . . ?"

Cameron's jaw twitched as he exhaled through his nose. "Father, this is Mavis. She's staying with me for a few days. Mavis, this is my father, Severin DeSalle."

"Is she now?" Severin asked, clearly affronted that Cameron hadn't cleared my stay with him first. "And for what reason are you staying with my son, Mavis?"

I lifted a brow at his presumption. Cam may have been afraid to stand up to his father, but I sure wasn't.

"Do you normally give out your personal information to a new acquaintance the first minute you meet them?" I asked him cheekily.

Severin's brown eyes flashed to black. "I am very old and very powerful, Mavis. My age, along with my stature in the demonic community, should secure a little respect from underlings such as yourself. You would do well to remember that."

His haughty tone made my cheeks flush hot with anger. "And you'd do well to remember that you have no idea who you're dealing with," I seethed. "You have no idea what I'm capable of. Maybe you should examine your own shitty behavior."

Cam's eyes widened in fear as his father took a step toward me and hissed, "Mind your tongue, you little wench, or I shall teach you manners myself!"

I narrowed my eyes at the insult and took a step closer to him, feeling calmer than I had in days as I boldly squared up with him. "Bring it, jackass."

Roaring in anger, Severin screamed, "You will respect me, demon!"

"If I do, you will have earned it, you fucking asshole!" I shot back, feeling a cold draft circle around us.

He clenched his fists to his sides as if he was struggling not to throttle me with his bare hands, and then he whirled on Cameron. "I'd like a word outside. Now."

Cameron pressed his lips together and followed his father, looking back at me with a *what the fuck* expression before he closed the door behind them.

I dropped to the couch, feeling numb. What had I just done? I was so angry over the high-handed way he'd treated me, I didn't stop to think how Severin might be tempted to take out his frustrations on his son.

After a few minutes, Cameron came back in wearing a shell-shocked expression. "You're not going to believe this," he said, "but my father liked you."

"You're kidding?" I asked, feeling a little shocked myself.

"When he asked me to go outside, I thought he was going to go apeshit, but he just laughed and said he'd like to shut you up by shoving his cock down your throat. There was a load of other graphic sexual threats, but I'll spare you those."

I screwed up my face in disgust. "Ew. Did he say anything else?"

"He asked if we were fucking."

My eyebrows shot up. "What did you tell him?"

"I told him we were. I may be able to get away with some important omissions, but my father can always tell when I'm lying. It's a skill he's perfected over his many years of manipulating humans."

"Exactly how many years has he been a douche?"

"Six hundred and something. I forget the exact number."

"Holy shit," I exclaimed. "No wonder he was pissed at me."

Cam sat down on the couch and pulled me into his lap. "I think he might have been more intrigued than pissed. I doubt anyone has talked to him like that since my mother was alive."

"I don't know. He didn't seem too intrigued to me."

"Trust me. He was."

"How could you tell?" I asked, relaxing into the warmth of his body.

"He told me."

"He told you he was intrigued. Like, he literally said he was intrigued by me?"

"He did . . . in so many words," he hedged.

I squinted at him. "What words?"

"He asked me to tell you to give him a call when you want to fuck a demon that can make his cock as big as you want it. Oh, and he said he'd be happy to teach you some discipline and respect in the most painful way possible."

"I think I'm going to puke," I said, feeling queasy.

"I think I'm a little scared to leave you here alone while I'm gone tomorrow."

"You're leaving?" I asked. "Where are you going?"

Cam leveled me with a stare. "Mavis, you know what I am and what I have to do."

"I do. But do you have to do it so soon?"

"If I want to keep my soul and pay my rent, yes."

I sighed and tried to keep the pout from my face. I didn't want to admit it, but I didn't feel any empathy for the women Cameron would bed; I only felt jealousy. As selfish as it was, I wanted him for myself and despised the thought of someone else enjoying what I considered mine and mine alone.

"You know I wouldn't go if I had another choice," he said, noticing my disquiet.

"I know," I admitted.

He kissed my forehead. "I know things are moving fast for us right now, but everything will settle soon. You'll be bored with me and my unchangeable dick in a month."

Reluctantly, I grinned at him. "It'll never happen."

AFTER A DELICIOUS DINNER from Napoli's, Cam and I decided to stretch our legs by taking a walk to the square to see the decorations being put up for the holiday. But though I was anxious to see the town while it had actual people milling about, I was concerned that we'd run into Cameron's father. I didn't think I was ready to see him so soon after hearing what his idea of a good time with me would be like.

I explained this fear to Cam as we started walking down Main Street, but he brushed off my concern with a laugh. "You have nothing to worry about. My father hasn't stayed for any real length of time in Havenwood Falls since the 1940s."

"Too many burnt bridges?" I asked, taking notice of a bar called the Haven Saloon on the corner and a store named Shelf Indulgence next door to it as we walked.

"Exactly."

"Why do you think he's such an asshat? What made him like this?"

Cam eyed the crowd of giggling teenagers walking toward us and slung an arm around me, pulling me closer to his side. "My father is a demon, Mavis. Being an asshat pretty much comes with the territory."

"But you aren't a jerk," I argued.

"I'm also half human," he pointed out. "Those of us lucky enough to have grown up outside of Hell, even the ones that aren't part human, are surprisingly tolerant. My father, on the other hand, has spent most of his time with demons."

"So, if demons raised me, I'd probably be the same."

"More than likely. Demons are not pleasant folk. They're rather like vampires who live in a nest. They feed off each other's angsty emotions."

"Vampires are real?" I asked, trying to keep my shocked voice low enough that none of the passersby would hear.

Cam pointed to a quaint gazebo covered with autumn décor on the far end of the square and laced his fingers with mine as we walked across the street to the opposite sidewalk. "You don't blink an eye at hearing there are other supernaturals, but you freak out about vampires?" he asked quietly.

"Yes!" I hissed. "I can't believe you thought this was the safest place for me! The town is full of monsters!"

"I *know* this is the safest place for you, Mavis. The resident monsters won't bother you. They probably won't even know you're a demon. That's the beauty of the tattoo you were given. It keeps our identities and our powers secret."

"So, there could be more demons in Havenwood Falls that you don't know about?"

"No. Remember, I've been in Havenwood Falls a very long time."

I let Cam lead me up the steps of the gazebo and leaned against a railing. "It's so easy to forget that you're a senior citizen."

He scoffed. "Senior citizen, indeed."

"Okay, maybe you're not that old, but there's no doubt you've seen a lot of things I couldn't imagine."

"It is true that I have seen my fair share of happenings in the town, but I mostly keep to myself. Penelope is one of the only residents I routinely spend time with."

"She seems nice."

"She is nice. She's been a great comfort to me for the past few years she's lived next door."

I eyed him speculatively. "How much of a comfort?"

He smiled, clearly enjoying seeing me jealous. "I haven't had sex with her, if that's what you're asking. Though my father does regularly ask me to steal her soul."

I gritted my teeth. "Severin is a dick."

Cam shrugged. "As I said, he's a demon. They all hunger for more of what they want—more power, more money, more souls, more sex—it's always something."

"I'm starting to realize how lucky I was to have found you on that road."

Wrapping his arms around me, he nuzzled his face into my hair. "I'm the lucky one, darling."

My eyes closed, and I breathed in his clean male scent. "I'm going to miss you, Cam. I wish you didn't have to go."

Pulling away to meet my eyes, he said, "You have no idea how much I want to stay."

"Then stay. Stay here with me."

"My father may change his mind about liking you if I stay."

"That is a chance I'm willing to take," I said, growing angry. I wasn't about to let some prick demon keep me from being with Cameron, father or not.

He tucked a lock of hair behind my ear. "It's not one I'm willing to take. I can't lose you, Mavis. I've grown rather fond of you."

My smile might have lit up the entire town when I heard those words come out of his mouth. He liked me. Cameron DeSalle liked me. And no matter what his occupation was or how controlling his father was, I knew I liked him back.

"Are you sure it's not the sex you're fond of?" I asked teasingly.

He narrowed his eyes at me. "That's not the response I expected."

I laughed and kissed his soft lips. "I'm rather fond of you, too, Cam. Never forget it."

He picked me up, and I squealed as he swung me around the

gazebo. When he settled me back on my feet, he kissed me until I was breathless then leaned his forehead against mine. "I will never forget."

CHAPTER 8

*a*n hour after our walk around the square, Cam and I lay curled up in his bed, our arms wound around each other as we talked. Both of us had happy, silly smiles plastered to our faces as we still reeled from our admissions of fondness.

It was hard to imagine anyone liking me the way he'd admitted to. Yes, I had had relationships before, but none of them were ever serious enough that I'd considered bringing them home to meet Leon, as antisocial as he was. But Cam—I would have been proud to take him back to meet my family. It was ironic that I felt that way now that I had no home to go to anymore.

I smiled at a goofy grin he was wearing as he stared at me and felt a sharp pain in my chest when I thought of him leaving the next day.

"Stop thinking about it," Cam said, pulling up the blankets and wrapping them tightly around us.

"Thinking about what?" I asked, trying to smooth out the telltale furrows on my forehead.

He returned to our cuddling position and ran a thumb across my worried face. "Me leaving tomorrow."

I sighed heavily. "How did you know?"

"It's forty below under these covers," he said, rolling on top of me to lick my cheek.

"Ew! Why did you do that?" I screeched, wiping his saliva from my skin.

"I wanted to see if my tongue would stick to you," he explained.

I shook my head. "You are a ridiculous demon."

"And you are a beautiful demon," he said, pressing his lips to mine.

I groaned and arched my body up to his. I could feel his searching hardness as I opened to him. He wanted me.

"You have far too many clothes on," I griped.

"I could say the same to you, you know."

"You're welcome to take them off," I said, sliding my hands up his shirt to explore the firm muscles of his back.

"I could," he said, smiling down at me.

I lifted a brow. "Well?"

He sighed and rolled off me, sitting up. "I can't right now. I have to make arrangements for that thing you keep thinking about, but don't want to talk about."

I sat up, my disappointment clear in my expression. "What kind of arrangements?"

"Some for me and some for you. I need to call the grocery store before they close to make sure you're able to add things to my tab, and I need to call Penelope and ask her to keep an eye on you."

"And for you?" I prompted.

"Hotel arrangements," he admitted, grudgingly. "And I need to confirm the appointment time with the client."

I pressed my lips together and stared down at my lap. I couldn't seem to make myself look at him.

"Don't worry about her, Mavis. These women mean nothing to me."

"They mean something to me," I retorted. "They're real people with souls I'm sure they'd like to keep."

He sighed and grabbed his laptop. Opening it, he powered it up and called me over to look at it. "This is Francesca Menish, Mavis. She's the woman I'm going to see tomorrow."

My eyes widened at the middle-aged woman with the soccer mom haircut. "She's not what I was expecting."

"You were expecting someone younger and more attractive?" he asked. "Someone more like yourself?"

I nodded.

"Darling, you have to understand that who I get for clients is beyond my control. I can't cherry-pick the young, attractive ones. And honestly, I rarely get anyone like that anyway. The women I fuck are usually middle-aged, and they're always married. They get bored with their husbands and go looking for someone who appears young and virile. Yes, I steal their souls, but they aren't shy young women being taken advantage of, Mavis. They pay me to be a whore, as they so often like to remind me, and I'm expected to do what I'm told."

I blanched. "That's . . . awful, Cam."

"It is, but this is my lot in life. And I've been living this life for a long, long time. I've grown accustomed to what my father expects, and in the whole scheme of things, it isn't so bad. I consider myself to be very fortunate. Some cambions have it much worse than I do. Some are slaves to their fathers. Some have never stepped foot out of the underworld. As evil as my father is, and as much as I despise him, he has never taken away my all of my independence, and I cannot be anything but thankful for that blessing."

"When you put it like that, your dad doesn't seem like such a dick."

"Oh, make no mistake. He's definitely a dick, but I'm worth more to him out here doing his bidding than I am in the underworld doing whatever the other cambions are tasked with."

"Have you ever been to the underworld?" I asked. "What's it like?"

"No, I haven't, and I hope never to have to go."

"I take it it's not a place I want to see."

"Absolutely not." He cupped my face. "I would die before I saw you go to the underworld, Mavis."

I circled his wrists with my hands and closed my eyes, just enjoying the feel of him touching me. "Let's hope it never comes to that, then."

I felt the bed dip down as he leaned in to kiss me. "Even if it does, Mavis, it would be worth it."

~

CAM LEFT EARLY the next morning, leaving me sad but completely spent and sore in his bed. I'd idly wondered aloud as he was getting dressed if he would be able to perform to his best ability after the hours we'd spent tangled up in each other's bodies the night before, but he'd just laughed and said that an infinitely hard cock was one of the incubus perks. I could certainly agree with that observation. He had rocked my world so hard, I'd passed out cold without even remembering it.

I languished in bed for a few hours, alternatively feeling happy and then regressing and crying bitter tears of hate. It made me so angry that Severin would make his son do this for him. And what made it so much worse was that there was no end date on this situation. Cam was saddled with this curse forever.

When I couldn't take lying in bed and doing nothing anymore, I showered, got dressed, and talked myself into going next door to visit with Penelope. Cam had mentioned more than a few times that he wanted me to become friendly with her, but I wasn't great at making friends and wasn't sure how to approach her. Would she even want to be friends with me?

By the way Penelope snatched the door open the second I knocked and exclaimed, "Finally!" I had to guess she did. Squealing, she grabbed my hand and dragged me into the apartment before I could explain that I was the demon she'd met before.

"Wow!" she said excitedly, showing me to the sofa. "You look so different without the horns!"

I had to laugh. "Those horns are hard to get used to, believe me."

"I'll bet. So what brings you by? I know you couldn't tell by my reaction at the door, but I really didn't expect you until later, especially after the grand send-off I overheard last night."

"I'm so sorry about that," I said, my cheeks growing hot. "I guess we need to look into some soundproofing?"

She waved away my embarrassment with a hand. "No way. I'm

living vicariously through you guys. I can't find anyone around here to touch my vagina with a ten-foot pole."

I guffawed. "That . . . sounds painful."

"I'm just telling you how it is. All these hot guys in this town and no one wants the boring human. It's either that, or they don't like the smell of Chinese."

"Huh?"

She giggled. "Sorry, that sounded weird. What I meant was that I work over at Sakura Buffet in Miller's Plaza. I come home smelling like sweet and sour pork five days a week."

"Do you like working there?"

She shrugged. "I have no complaints, other than the food smells embedded in my clothes. It pays the bills, and it could be worse."

"Yeah, you could have Cam's job," I said with more than a little vitriol in my voice.

"Yes!" she shouted, throwing up a fist. "I was hoping we were going to talk about this."

I sighed and relaxed back onto some of the fluffy colorful throw pillows she had scattered around the sofa and chairs. "I hate it, Penelope. Thinking about him out there with some other woman, it makes me irrationally angry."

"I don't think it's too irrational. You like him, right?"

"It seems weird to say that so soon, but yeah, I do like him, and he says he's fond of me."

"I don't doubt it. Do you know how many times he's asked me to watch over one of his lovers?"

"No. How many?"

"None."

"None?"

"None," she assured me. "I have never once seen Cameron bring any female home, demon or otherwise. He always said he was fine being alone, that he didn't want to subject anyone to his father or his lifestyle of prostitution."

"Prostitution . . ." I shook my head and stared at my hands. "I never thought I'd be dating someone involved in the oldest profession."

"And I never thought I'd be best friends with a prostitute, but here we are."

"Do you think he hates the sex with those women?"

She blew out a raspberry. "No. Well, maybe he will now. But before you, that was the only sex he was getting, so he looked forward to fucking something other than his hand."

We stared at each other, then burst into helpless giggles.

"I'm sorry," I said, trying to pull myself together. "I just have a hard time believing that someone as good-looking as Cam would only be having sex with himself."

"It is rather unbelievable, and honestly, if I didn't have to listen to him whine about it for the past few years, I wouldn't believe it. He is gorgeous, isn't he?"

I smiled, thinking of Cam's handsome face. "He really is, but he must look like his mom. Severin didn't look much like him."

"I'd be scared to see what his father really looks like. Severin isn't human, remember? That form he takes when he comes into town is just a manifestation of what he thinks is most pleasing to the eye of a human woman."

I frowned. I couldn't believe I'd forgotten that so quickly. "I guess I'm not used to this whole demon thing yet."

"Yeah, about that," she said, getting up to join me on the sofa. "How is it possible that you hadn't seen your demon form until yesterday?"

I started to answer, but then wondered if that was a smart course to take. Cam said Penelope could be trusted, but could I tell her something as big as the truth about myself? What if she wasn't as trustworthy as he believed? What if she somehow knew Leon LeGrand and would alert him to my whereabouts?

I sighed, mentally slapping myself. I was being silly. Penelope was a human. What would she know about the whole Exitium Daemonium thing?

Finally, I summoned up my nerve and said, "It's a long story."

"I have leftover Kung Pao Chicken. Want to heat some up and talk demon shit?"

I laughed at her composure with the "demon shit" and nodded. "Sounds good."

Penelope clapped her hands and danced to the kitchen door, her waist-length brown hair swinging behind her. I stood and followed her into the kitchen, taking a seat on a barstool at the counter.

"So," she began, measuring out equal scoops of fragrant chicken and vegetables onto two plates. "Let's hear your story."

I took a deep breath. "I found out I was an ice demon three days ago."

She stopped spooning. "Three days?"

"Yeah, I fell down a flight of concrete steps at the library and had to go to the hospital."

"Ouch."

"That was only half as painful as what I found out later."

She put the first plate in the microwave and set it for two minutes. "What did you find out?"

"That I'm some demon-killing machine called the Exitium Daemonium."

"You're a demon killer? And Cam, a demon, brought you home to stay with him?" She laughed. "Well, he's an idiot."

"I didn't give him a lot of choices. He found me hiding from my fake grandfather in a ditch."

"This story gets weirder and weirder," she commented, opening the microwave to switch the plates. "But go on."

"Basically, when I went in for x-rays at the hospital, there was this diamond-shaped thing in my chest covered with runes—runes that I had seen on journals in my grandfather's study."

"Creepy!" she blurted out, handing me a plate and a fork.

"Creepier than you know," I agreed, forking a bite and attempting to cool it without freezing it to the spoon.

She leaned on the counter. "So, what do the runes mean?"

I shrugged. "From what Cam and I can figure out, they were some spell to keep my power throttled. Obviously, the demon masquerading as my grandfather wanted to keep me from knowing I was anything but one hundred percent human."

"Obviously," she agreed. "What did the journals say? I assume that's how you found out your grandfather was fake."

I nodded, chewing thoughtfully. "I only read one all the way through, but it basically was an account of how this demon, Leon LeGrand, was tasked with stealing me from the underworld and raising me as a human until he would use me to kill every demon that stood in the way of his master."

Enthralled by the story, Penelope ignored the beeping microwave. "Who's his master?"

"I don't know. I ran out of the house as soon as I could grab a few changes of clothes and money."

"Wow."

I nodded, "When you saw me yesterday, that was when I realized the throttle wasn't working anymore. I've been practicing a little with the ice thing since then, but the demon killing, not so much."

"Yeah, that you might want to keep under wraps, especially when Cam is home."

"Trust me. Cam is the last demon I want to kill."

She smirked at me knowingly. "I wouldn't want to kill the demon giving me all those orgasms either."

CHAPTER 9

Though I warned her I didn't have much cash, Penelope insisted we go to Miller's Plaza to shop for what she called "Netflix supplies" after our meal. I didn't argue. Going to the store with her would give me a chance to check out more of the town. Plus, I was learning a lot about Cam and his habits, likes, and dislikes as she chatted good-naturedly. It was clear they'd been friends a very long time.

But once we pulled into the parking lot, I knew Penelope had more up her sleeve than grocery shopping.

"What are you to?" I asked, staring at the windows draped in red curtains and the telltale sign proclaiming the business in front of us was called Pleasurez.

A slow smile spread across her face as she realized I was on to her. "Whatever do you mean, Mavis?"

"You know exactly what I mean, Penelope. Pleasurez? Really?"

"Yes, really! Don't you want to get something sexy to show Cam what he's been missing while he's been gone? You don't think those women are wearing something sexy for him?"

"If there's anything decent and good in this world, they're all wearing bloomers," I told her, grimacing at the thought.

"Come on," she said, opening her door. "Just humor me. Remember, I'm living vicariously through you. I *need* this."

I rolled my eyes and met her in front of the car. "We have to find you a man before this gets any weirder."

"Preaching to the choir, sister," she said, throwing a hand up to the heavens. "From your mouth to God's ears."

"Let's just do this," I said, gritting my teeth and opening the door for Penelope, who was wearing a supremely patronizing smirk as she sauntered past me.

Upon entering the store, I stopped still, immediately daunted by the sheer number of things to look at. It was all tastefully done, of course, but to a girl who had never been in this kind of place, it was just north of overwhelming and just south of "what the hell am I doing here?"

"Oh my gosh!" Penelope squealed, running up to a mannequin wearing an open-crotched, see-through lace bodysuit that left absolutely nothing to the imagination. "This would be gorgeous on you!"

I checked the price tag. "Wouldn't it be cheaper if I just showed up naked? I'm pretty sure things will still go in the right direction."

"Mavis!" she whined. "Let me enjoy this!"

"If you need something to enjoy, might I suggest one of those glass dildos on the table over there and some of this garishly pink strawberry lube?"

She glared at me and grabbed a size small from the rack. "Take this to the nice lady and tell her to wrap it up. I'm buying it."

"Fine," I said, sighing at her insistence. "But just so you know, I'm going to be really quiet next time and you'll never even know that we're doing it."

She pouted. "You suck."

"And you need a boyfriend . . . badly."

ONCE WE WERE BACK at her apartment with the lingerie and enough Twizzlers and Sour Patch Kids to sugar up all the kids in town, we watched most of season four of *Supernatural*. Penelope said it wasn't worth watching until Castiel's character joined the show, and I couldn't disagree. I didn't think she'd let me. She was a colossal Castiel fan.

Around ten o'clock, Cam texted Penelope, worried when he couldn't get me on the home phone. She berated him for interrupting her bingeing and passed the phone to me with a loud, "IT'S YOUR LOVERBOY!"

I rolled my eyes and put the phone up to my ear. "Hello?"

"Hey, baby."

I melted a little bit when I heard his smooth, sexy voice. "Hey, yourself. How's it going?"

"I was going to ask the same. What are you and Penelope up to?"

"Watching *Supernatural*."

He chuckled. "Of course you are. She's been pissed at me for months for saying Crowley was the best character. She refuses to watch the show with me now."

"That sounds . . . accurate," I told him, grinning at the way Penelope was kissing her fingers and pressing them to Misha Collins's lips when he was on the screen.

"You have no idea."

I laughed. "So where are you calling from?"

"Cheyenne."

"Wyoming?"

He sighed. "Yes, and it's every bit as exciting as it sounds."

"I don't want to hear how exciting it is," I muttered.

"Darling, you won't ever hear about that."

"Thank God for small favors. So, when can I expect you back?"

"Sometime around midday tomorrow, or sooner, if I can get away."

"Good," I told him.

"You're sulking. I can hear it in your voice."

"Do you blame me? You just traveled to Cheyenne to fuck some middle-aged married lady who probably drives a minivan."

"Oh, damn!" Penelope yelled, laughing her ass off. "I like her, Cam!"

"And I'm second-guessing introducing you two," he responded. "I don't think I thought it through."

"Hey, you brought this on yourself," I told him. "I can't help it if you have good taste in friends."

"You'd better not be saying anything disparaging about me, asshole," Penelope yelled. "Not you, Castiel," she added, blowing a kiss to her favorite TV angel.

As if he could hear my train of thought, he said, "She's obsessed."

"If only you could find an angel for her here on Earth."

He didn't answer.

"Cam, please don't tell me there are angels here in Havenwood Falls."

"Okay, I won't."

"I can't tell if you're kidding when you're not here."

"I don't think you can tell when I *am* there."

"Yes, I can. You blink a lot when you lie."

"Are you teasing me?" he asked, his voice suspicious.

"Maybe," I sing-songed.

Cam laughed. "I really do miss you, you sassy thing."

"I miss you, too, ridiculous demon."

"Then I'll see you tomorrow?" he asked.

"If you plan on coming home, you will," I answered.

He groaned. "Go home soon. You're already starting to pick up Penelope's snark."

"Yes, sir."

"Bye, darling."

I handed the phone back to Penelope and tried to wipe the silly smile off my face before she saw it.

"You guys are adorable," she said, grinning at me from the floor. "I'm glad he picked you up from that ditch."

"Girl, you and me both."

69

~

I EXCUSED myself to go home at daybreak, which coincided with the time Penelope started to nod off into a bowl of Skittles, and walked back to the apartment feeling excited about seeing Cameron soon. At first, I thought it would upset me, knowing what he'd been out doing with another woman, but now I had a feeling I would just be glad to see him come home safe . . . if he showered for a couple of hours after.

When I unlocked the door to the apartment, I almost turned around and went back to Penelope's when I caught a whiff of unfamiliar aftershave, but I convinced myself that I was imagining things. The door was locked with a deadbolt, and there were no windows accessible from the outside. Cam had assured me I'd be perfectly safe by pointing that out before he left.

Brushing off my fears, I showered, shaved my legs, and spent extra time blow drying my hair, so I wouldn't appear as if I stuck my finger in every light socket in the apartment while he was gone. Dressing in the cute panties and bra set I'd bought at Pleasurez, I wiped down the foggy mirror on the back of the bathroom door and looked at myself at every angle. Risqué lingerie wasn't really my thing, but I had to admit, I looked damn good in this getup. Yawning, I smiled at myself and opened the door, ready to climb in bed for a few hours of sleep before Cam got home.

The moment I opened the door, I heard a low whistle. Twirling around, I came face to face with a tall blond man I'd never seen before.

"Who are you?" I asked, covering myself with my hands as best as I could.

"Leon LeGrand sent me to get you," he said, his cold blue eyes lewdly raking up and down my barely covered body. "But I don't think he'd mind if I were a little late getting you back to Utah. He didn't mention what a tasty little tart you are."

I backed away a few steps. "I don't know who you're talking about," I lied. "I don't know any Leon LeGrand."

"Oh," he asked, pulling my backpack from behind him. "This isn't your wallet in here with a Utah ID that has your picture on it? I have to say, the picture does not do you justice."

"You need to leave before I call the police," I said, my voice trembling.

"How are you going to call them? With the phone in the kitchen? You know, Cameron DeSalle called for you earlier on that phone. I traced the number to Wyoming. Is your half-human lover in Wyoming, sweet thing? Did he leave you here by yourself?"

I didn't answer. I couldn't explain. I was using every bit of my brainpower to try to maneuver myself out of this situation. I was not getting raped today or ever.

"Look," I said finally. "I'm not going back to Leon. You've come all this way for nothing."

His lascivious, nauseating smile ratcheted up as he stared at the breasts spilling out of my demicup bra. "I wouldn't say it was for nothing."

Taking another step back, I concentrated as hard as I could on making my power come to life. I needed a weapon, something I could throw or attack him with, but there was nothing.

He took a step closer. "Come on, baby. Let's have a little fun before I take you back to Utah."

"Get away from me!" I screamed, throwing my arms out in front of me.

"Hey!" he yelled, ducking under the icicles I unknowingly slung at him. He straightened. "That wasn't very nice, Mavis."

"I said, get away from me!" I yelled back. I was done with this guy causing me trouble. I was in my demon form now. I could feel the weight of my horns on top of my head and the ice ready to go at my fingertips.

The man stepped back a few steps and held up his hands in a defensive motion. "Whoa, now. Just calm down."

"Get the fuck out!" I bellowed at him, swallowing hard when a pain shot through my chest.

"I will," he said, inching his way closer to the front door.

I took a menacing step toward him. "Then go!"

Just then, the door swung open, and Penelope stormed in with an aluminum baseball bat. She took in the man facing me with his hands up and me in in my demon form and lingerie. "What the fuck is going on in here?"

The stranger didn't wait a beat. He lunged for the bat, wrestling it from Penelope's hands and shoving her into the corner all in one movement before slamming the front door shut.

"Well, well, well," he said, looking positively giddy at the turn of events. "Looks like it's my lucky day." He examined the baseball bat and continued. "Now ladies, I think we should all calm down, and then you can figure it out amongst yourselves which of you will be sucking my dick first."

Penelope let loose with a tirade like I'd never heard before when he finished his revolting speech, standing up tall in the corner and looking like she'd rip him apart with her bare hands. I just stared at the action playing out in front of me, a wave of calm flowing over me, seconds before I walked up to the surprised man and laid my frozen pale hands on his arm. I had no idea what I was doing. I just instinctively knew that was what I needed to do.

The man screamed as a glowing white light engulfed his arm and spread out like wildfire across his body. His screams grew louder and louder until he seemed to come to a breaking point. Like, a literal breaking point. As soon as his screams cut off, the white light expanded into every nook and cranny of the apartment, and he exploded into a million minuscule pieces of demon.

CHAPTER 10

When the light of my magic had faded, and every bit of what was left of the stranger had settled onto the carpet, I sank to my knees. I had killed someone. It was true that he might've hurt Penelope or me, but did he really deserve a fate as awful as what I'd done to him?

"I know what you're thinking, Mavis," Penelope said softly. "You did what you had to. He could have raped and killed both of us. His death was justified."

I looked up at her with tears streaming down my cheeks. "I don't know what I did."

She crouched down next to me and threw her arms around me, hugging me tightly. "You did what you had to."

I held onto her, utterly adrift. I felt like I was riding the line between dreaming and wakefulness. None of this could be real. Would I wake up tomorrow safely tucked into my childhood bed, all of this a dream?

Looking around me, I knew that wouldn't be the case. There was no way my brain came up with something as real and vivid as this.

"Oh my God," I said, breaking away from her. "We have to clean this up. Cam can't come home to this."

"I'm on it," she said, jumping to her feet. "Give me two seconds."

I nodded stiffly and stayed put as she ran out the front door.

Seconds after she left, I heard her say, "Hi, Mrs. Woods!" then she laughed. "Nope, there's no one getting murdered in there. We had a blender explosion with our raspberry smoothies. I keep telling Cam to let me use the appliances, but you know he never listens." Another laugh. "Yes, ma'am. See you later. Say hi to Jordan for me."

Sighing with relief, I got to my feet and surveyed the mess. It wasn't as bad as I'd thought it was going to be. The worst of it was the blood stain, but the rest of the organs and bones seemed to have disintegrated in the explosion.

Penelope came back in the door a moment later with a wet-dry vacuum and two huge bottles of hydrogen peroxide.

"You're lucky I buy in bulk," she said, handing me the bottle tucked under her arm.

"I'm lucky you showed up. I don't know what would've happened if you didn't."

She stared down at what was left of the man and laughed. "You don't?"

My lips twitched. "Don't make me laugh. This is serious."

"Yeah, seriously awesome. Dude, can you do this to my ex-boyfriend?"

"I'm not even sure what I did." I jerked my gaze to her. "What if you had been a demon? I could have killed you with that light thing, too."

"I don't think so," she said. "I couldn't even feel it when the light covered me."

"But that could have been because you're a human. What if it just works on demons? Oh, fuck! What if I accidentally do this to Cameron? What am I going to do, Penelope? I can't hurt him."

She put down the vacuum and slapped me. "You're hysterical, Mavis. Calm down."

"Hey!" I said, holding my cheek.

She threw her hands up. "Sorry, I'm a little hysterical, too. This is crazy pants territory, you know?"

Leaning down with my hands on my knees, I closed my eyes and took in a slow breath, counting down and holding it in like Cam showed me. Slowly, I opened my eyes as I blew out the breath and was relieved to find I was calmer.

"Better?" Penelope asked, her lips quirked up in a half smile.

I straightened. "Much."

"Good, go fill this reservoir with hot water for me. I'll vacuum up the . . . bits."

I took the plastic basin to the kitchen and turned on the tap, waiting for it to warm. Sighing heavily, I held my hand under the water and let my mind wander. I couldn't believe what was happening. An hour ago, I was happily watching Sam and Dean Winchester figure out where all the reapers had run off to, and now I was meting out death like I was one of them.

When the tank was full, I carefully took it back out to a severely disgusted Penelope.

"This is so gross," she told me. "We need to figure out how you can do this without the mess."

"I'm not doing this again," I said sternly. "Ever."

"Never?" she asked skeptically, holding up a bloody cell phone and a wallet. "What if I told you this guy had the number of one Mr. Leon LeGrand in his contacts?"

"I knew Leon sent him," I admitted. "He told me."

"What in the name of Hell is going on in here?" Cam asked, striding into the apartment. His face was thunderous and terrible in its beauty as he took in my state of undress, the baseball bat, and the bloodstain in the middle of the living room carpet. "Someone tell me why the Court is blowing up my phone. Now."

"I think that's my cue to leave," Penelope said, handing me the vacuum handle. "Call me, Mavis."

"Wait," Cam demanded.

She stopped just short of the door and whispered, "So close."

"I did it," I told him. "It was me."

He looked to the floor then back to me. "What is this?"

Penelope piped up. "Franco Ross is what his license says."

"And why is Franco Ross now a stain on my freshly shampooed carpet?"

"Because I'm the Exitium Daemonium?" I asked.

The shock on his face was understandable as he looked me over for injuries. "You did this with your power?"

I nodded. "I threw an icicle at him first, but he ducked out of the way."

He pinched the bridge of his nose, sighed, and then pulled me into his arms to bury his face in my hair. "Was it Leon who sent him?" he asked.

"Yes."

His grip tightened. "I'm sorry I left you. If I had known, I would have never left you. I thought you'd be safe here."

"It's not your fault, Cam," I said, stroking his dark hair with shaky hands. "You couldn't have known. And it's not like you can babysit me forever. At some point, we were going to have to continue living our lives."

When he pulled back, his eyes were black. "I will not rest until Leon LeGrand is dead. Fuck my father and this job. I have money saved. I can take off as long as it takes to finish him."

"You don't even know where he is."

"Utah is a pretty good guess."

"Stop being stubborn and listen to me, Cam. You're not going to risk your soul to sit around and wait for nothing to happen. That's your emotions talking. Once you're calm and we have Mr. Ross out of the carpet, maybe then cooler heads will prevail, and we can move on responsibly."

"Maybe," he agreed, grudgingly. "But first, can you tell me why you're wearing sexy lingerie to commit your first murder?"

CAM KICKED Penelope out and sent me to shower after we told him everything that had happened. I went willingly and without argument.

Though I felt bad that he insisted on cleaning up what was essentially a crime scene of my own making, his face told me he would brook no opposition. Secretly, I was relieved. I desperately wanted to get the sticky lingerie off my body, and maybe to burn it at the first opportunity.

Cam joined me in the bathroom twenty minutes after I got in the shower. I was still washing my hair. I'd washed it five times already, but I didn't feel clean. I wasn't sure I'd ever feel clean again.

"Are you okay?" he asked me through the clear shower door.

I nodded. "I think so. Are you?"

He pulled his shirt over his head and threw it in the hamper along with his pants and boxer briefs. "No, and I'm going to have to buy Penelope a new vacuum cleaner."

"I'm really sorry," I told him, sniffling a little. "It just happened."

He slid back the shower door and joined me under the spray. "Don't worry about it. I've taken care of it with the Court."

"How?" I asked, a little dubious. Cam might be a demon, but as far as demons went, he was on the weaker side. Even if he wasn't half human, incubuses had one type of magic and could only really hurt someone who had a soul.

"I do have some tricks up my sleeve, darling. I'm not as feeble as you think I am."

I frowned at him. "I do not think you're feeble. I just don't know how you could go up against Leon without some sort of demon-killing weapon."

He stilled my hand when I reached for the shampoo bottle again. "I do have a demon-killing weapon."

"You do?"

He nodded. "Mavis, you don't survive being a half human demon for a century without some survival skills and a weapon. I try to live an uncomplicated life here, but I am prepared."

"So what do you think we should do? We could leave town for a while," I suggested. "He can't find me if he doesn't know where to look."

"We're not leaving town. We're not going to run away from this.

We're immortal, Mavis. Do you want to be on the run for an eternity?"

"No, of course not. I just meant for a couple of weeks. Surely, Leon will come in the next few days if he knows where we are. If he sees we're not here, he'll begin searching somewhere else, and we can come home."

He pondered what I'd said as he soaped up his chest and rinsed off. "I'll consider it, but I don't like the idea of running. The Court is protecting you here. We don't know what we're up against outside the town limits."

I leaned my cheek against his smooth, clean chest and hugged him. "I'm glad you're home."

He wrapped his arms around me and squeezed. "I don't know what I would've done if Mr. Ross would've managed to steal you away from me, Mavis. I can't lose you."

Cam ushered me into his bed after we'd toweled off. I didn't have the strength to fight his wishes. Without getting any sleep the night before and all the excitement the morning had brought with it, I was exhausted. Apparently, eating a pound of gummy worms, watching mindless TV, and killing a stranger took a lot out of a demoness.

I snuggled right up to Cam when he joined me and sighed contentedly. He was warm and safe, and I knew, without a doubt, that I could trust him to protect me to the best of his ability.

"Did I mention how much I missed you?" I asked, kissing his chest.

He kissed the top of my head. "You couldn't have missed me half as much as I missed you. Every second away from you was torture."

I lifted my head to look at him. His chocolate brown eyes were full of an emotion I'd never seen in them before. "Are you positive about that? I have been nothing but trouble for you since the moment you found me in that ditch."

"That moment was the best moment of my life. I didn't realize it at the time, but my life had become monotonous and mundane. Finding you made me feel like I had a purpose, a reason to get out of bed in the morning."

"Ditto," I told him, pressing my lips to his. "You're the best thing that's ever happened to me."

He grinned, a little of his personality shining through the gloom of the situation. "You just like my fun stick."

I shook my head. "Nah."

Eyes narrowing, he rolled me onto my back and hovered over me, his cock heavy against my most intimate part.

"You want to try that again?" he asked. "This time you might want to say it in a more believable voice."

I laughed, then hissed as the movement pushed his hard sex against me. "You'd better be careful with that thing."

"How careful do you want it?" he asked, a telling smirk on his face.

"Very careful," I answered, opening my legs to him. "I like . . ."

"Shh," he interrupted, moving down on the bed and kissing each thigh before catching my eye with his smoldering ones and grinning like the devil incarnate. His hot breath made me shiver in anticipation.

"Please," I begged, aching to feel that first sweet sensation. "Please, touch me."

Nodding, he slipped his muscled arm across my stomach and took a firm grip on my hip, letting me know exactly who was in control.

And me? I could only pant, my anticipation sending every nerve in my body on high alert. "Fuck, Cam," I breathed out. "If you don't touch me soon, I'm going to start hyperventilating."

He chuckled and lowered his head, rasping his tongue slow and steady against my clit. It was a testing, teasing stroke, one that made me cry out with embarrassing relief, and when he repeated the motion, I couldn't stop myself from convulsing and arching up to press myself to his mouth. There was no grace, no shyness. At that moment, there was nothing but pure need.

"Please," I begged again, twisting my fingers into his hair.

Cam slid his body up, settling between my legs, and kissed me, thrusting his tongue into my mouth. I groaned as I tasted myself and matched his movements, abandoning all pretense of restraint. Every bit of my focus was on that kiss, every bit of my hunger. I wanted him, wanted what he could give me. And I wanted it badly. He growled, breaking away and sitting up on his knees. I stared at his massive erection longingly, wanting so much to feel him inside me.

"See something you want, darling?" he asked teasingly.

I poked my bottom lip out in a pout. "You know what I want."

"Careful, darling. I'll bite that lip while I'm showing you how fun this cock can be."

I met his nearly black eyes with my own. "Bring it, big boy."

Cam dove for my mouth, biting, licking, sucking until my lips felt bruised and swollen. I didn't care. Nor did I care when he pushed into me hard and without warning. I dug my nails into his back and cried out for more. The action only seemed to spur him on. Lifting my legs over his shoulders, he cupped my breasts, pinching the nipples hard as he unmercifully pounded into me. He filled me over and over until I screamed out his name and a few other things that were certain to make even an incubus blush. Moments later, he roared with his release, pulling out of me and pumping his slick cock with his hand until he spilled all over my breasts.

Breathing hard, he collapsed next to me and handed me a discarded T-shirt to clean up. "Holy fuck," he said.

I laughed as I sat up and wiped myself dry. Dropping the shirt off the side of the bed, I rolled over to him and nestled in his arms. "I take it back. I do like your fun stick."

He chuckled and yawned. "I knew it."

CHAPTER 11

*C*am and I spent the next couple of days putting security measures in place and generally readying the apartment for anything crazy that might happen. For the moment, there was nothing else to be done. We could only wait for Leon to show up so that we or the Court could take care of him as quietly as possible and move on with our lives.

But as much as I was ready to do just that, Cam was dead set against me getting involved in the fight. And as much as I appreciated his overprotectiveness, I knew in my heart the only way to defeat Leon was to serve him the same justice I'd served Mr. Ross. He had to die to secure my safety. It was nonnegotiable, and that wasn't something I was sure a half incubus could accomplish on his own.

"What are you thinking about?" Cam asked me late one afternoon. He sat next to me on his couch and pulled me into his lap. "Your face is all scrunched up in concentration."

"Nothing you want to hear about," I assured him, thinking about his father. I'd been thinking about him a lot lately. Now that the demons searching for me had somehow infiltrated the town, I knew some of them could possibly talk to demons that were still loyal to Severin. Cam had said he had burnt his bridges in town, but I wasn't so sure. If Severin found out Cam had been hiding a prize like the

Exitium Daemonium under his nose, he might take me away, and possibly take Cam's soul in the process. I couldn't let that happen.

He sighed and curled a lock of my blond hair around his finger. "You need a break from all this."

"I do?"

"Yes, and I think I know just the thing."

"What's that?"

"It's been snowing all night."

I furrowed my brow. "And that should excite me because . . . ?"

"Because you're an ice demon? I thought it might be fun to take a walk in your element."

I grimaced and slipped off my sneakers in favor of a pair of boots. "Do you think it's safe for me out there?"

"Safer than it is in here. No one is going to look for you in the mountains."

"We're going up the mountain?"

"Just a short way up Mt. Sousa. You can't practice your power in town, Mavis. The tattoo doesn't protect humans from seeing that."

"But won't someone see us out there?" I asked, lacing up my boots.

"It's not very likely. I'm taking you to a spot that's usually pretty isolated."

I smiled at Cam, determined to not ruin this for both of us. We'd been using sex to fight off cabin fever for days. It was time to get out of our cell for a breath of fresh air. "Sounds good. Do you think Penelope will have a coat I can borrow?"

Cam grinned at my forgetfulness. "How many ice demons need a coat?"

"Oh," I said, blushing. "Then I guess I'm ready when you are."

He slipped on a black formfitting coat and turned back to me, looking so mouthwatering, it made me weak at the knees. "I'm ready."

"We'd better go or else I'll be dragging you into the bedroom. I've never seen anyone look as good in a coat as you do."

"That's because you've never seen anyone as good-looking as me," he said. "Damn these magnificent incubus genes. I'm just too irresistible for words."

"I know, I know," I said, blowing out a very put-upon sigh. "Hotness comes with the territory."

He bent down and laid a not-so-chaste kiss on my lips. "If we don't leave now, I'm the one that's not going to be able to keep myself from taking you to the bedroom."

"Don't think I'll tell you no," I countered.

"Some days I'm not sure which of us has the incubus parentage," he said, retaking my mouth, this time in an all-out assault as he kissed me deeply, thrusting his tongue inside.

I gasped in surprise at his urgency and groaned into his mouth as he palmed my breasts and pinched the nipples just hard enough to make me moan.

Cam pulled away. "Let's go, darling. I can't be alone in this apartment with you without wanting to sink my cock into that hot, wet pussy of yours."

I lifted my eyebrows in surprise. "That sure doesn't sound like you want to go."

He groaned and put more distance between us. "Come on. We need to get the hell out of here."

CAM and I left his apartment, walking briskly down Eighth Street in the late morning sun and paying attention to nothing but one another until we reached the other side of the town square. I had meant to take in more of the town that I hadn't seen on trips out before, but I couldn't seem to keep my eyes off him. He appeared to be suffering from the same problem. Every time I looked at him, he was staring back at me, his eyes alight with lust and something I couldn't place. Pride, maybe?

"Come here," he said, pulling me toward a small coffee shop on the corner of Stuart and Eighth Street. "It's freezing out here. I need something to warm me up."

"I may know a way to warm you up," I purred. "As a matter of fact, I think it could make you hot."

His eyes flared at my blatantly sexual remark. "Do you, little demon?"

"Once I get you away from the town, I just might have to show you."

He groaned as he discreetly adjusted his erection under his coat. "Come on, darling, let's go in before you get us both in trouble."

Smirking, I allowed Cam to usher me into the coffee shop, knowing it was just prolonging the inevitable sexual encounter we'd be having on Mt. Sousa. I couldn't keep my hands off his body, just like he couldn't stay away from mine. Honestly, I thought the town was lucky we hadn't christened every surface in the square with our escapades.

Broastful Brew was darker and quieter than I'd expected it to be, but it was cozy and warm as we stepped inside and wiped our feet on the door mat. An older woman Cam quickly identified as Mabel welcomed us with an energetic "HELLO!" that seemed out of place with the hushed tones of the rest of the patrons, who looked up to see who the newcomers were, then ducked their heads back into their conversations.

"Hello, Miss Mabel," Cam said, smiling pleasantly. "Two coffees to go, please."

"Coming right up!" She buzzed around the counter and pulled out two cups, filling them quickly and expertly.

Bemused, Cam said, "Miss Mabel, I don't think I've introduced you to my girlfriend, Mavis."

She grinned up at Cameron. "I should say not! I think I'd remember you bringing a girl in here." Turning to me, she added, "Nice to meet you, Mavis! How are you liking our quaint little town?"

"I'm liking it just fine," I told her. "It's so beautiful here with all the festive fall decorations."

"That it is," she agreed, happily putting the lids on the cups. "You should see this place around Christmas, when it's all snowy and lit up. It's really something then."

Handing over a ten-dollar bill, Cam told Mabel to keep the change and handed me one of the cups. "Well, we'd better get going. I'm taking her up Mt. Sousa to see the sights this morning."

Mabel clapped her hands together. "Oh, you'll love it, Mavis! The fresh fallen snow on the mountain is one of the best sights in the world! But you be sure to borrow this young man's coat if it gets too cold. I don't know what he's thinking, letting you traipse around town without one."

I grinned at her. "I will, Miss Mabel."

"Have a great day, you two!"

"She was really nice," I commented, once we were back on the sidewalk.

He nodded. "You know what else is nice?"

"What's that?"

"Thinking about the ways you'll warm me up on that mountain."

I shivered, my body heating up with desire. "You keep that talk up, and I'm going to be hot enough for the both of us."

His smile was pure sex. "I like the sound of that."

We continued our eye-fucking all the way to the base of the mountain and down a lengthy trail that led to a clearing so small, I would have missed it if Cam didn't point it out. Looking at the dense, snow-covered trees around us, I smiled. "It looks like a Christmas card. It's beautiful."

"You're beautiful," he said, cupping my face and kissing me softly.

Ignoring the compliment, I grinned and walked him back to the nearest tree. Sinking to my knees in front of him, I unbuckled his belt and unbuttoned his jeans, my breath catching as his cock sprang out hard and huge in my hands. "Oh, I am going to enjoy this."

Teeth clenched, he growled and stilled my hands.

"Not right now, you won't," he said, disbelief peppering his voice.

"Are you sure?" I asked, my heart thumping loudly in my ears.

He shook his head. "I'm not sure of anything right now."

"Good," I said, taking that as a yes and licking his cock from base to tip before taking it into my mouth as far as it would go.

Cam gripped my short ponytail and pumped himself into my mouth, taking control. "Fuck, Mavis," he groaned. "Suck my cock."

I happily obliged, alternating between letting him fuck my mouth and sucking him hard, using my teeth and hands to heighten the sensations.

I was so thoroughly engrossed in the task at hand, using Cam's grunts and moans as a guide, I didn't hear anyone approaching until a tree branch cracked and a voice asked, "Mavis, my love, do you mind telling me why you have that filthy human's cock in your mouth and what has become of my associate, Mr. Ross?"

CHAPTER 12

*T*he second I heard Leon LeGrand's voice, my demon form shot to the surface. Freezing stock still, I knew what I'd find when I turned to the sound, and I was right. Standing before us was the same black-suited, gray-haired man I'd come to know so well over the years.

Cam took one look at my transformation, and his handsome features ran the gamut from confusion to understanding and, finally, to murderous. Turning to face Leon, he zipped up his pants, stepped in front of me protectively, and growled, "He's mine."

Leon laughed heartily. "What are you going to do, cambion? Fuck me to death? You have no power over me."

I laid a hand on Cam's shoulder to calm him. "He may be a weaker demon than you, Leon, but I'm not. You'd do well to say your goodbyes now."

"Oh, so you've figured out what you are, have you?" His condescending tone made me want to stake him in the chest with an icicle. "Congratulations, granddaughter."

"Don't you fucking call me that," I spat. "You're less than nothing to me."

"Well, I can't say I'm disappointed that charade is over. I was sick of you by the time you were twelve years old. I never saw what was so special about you."

"Good. Then you won't be surprised when I end you. What do you think, Cam? I'm thinking icicles through his eyes and heart might be the most poetic."

"You little idiot. Ice will not affect me. I, myself, am an ice demon."

"No?" I asked. "Then let's see how you fare with my little secret."

Leon's eyes widened. "What do you mean, Mavis?"

My grin was sharp. "What do you think I mean, *grandfather*?"

"Is that what you did to Franco? You used your other power?"

I laughed. "I'm not some evil overlord who will tell all of her plans and devious deeds before you're miraculously saved by a hero, Leon. You won't be saved tonight. And I do not need to tell you what happened to your associate or to prolong your death."

I stepped forward, and Cam jerked me back to his side. "No, Mavis. I don't think he's alone."

The grin spread across Leon's face told me Cam was right. He wasn't alone.

"Who's here with you?" I demanded. "Or maybe a better question would be, do they know what I can do. Because I can promise you, Leon, if they are aligned with your cause, I will have no qualms about killing them, too."

"Mavis, Mavis, Mavis," he began. "I don't want to have to hurt you or your incubus lover. Come quietly with me, and I will let both of you live."

My shrill laugh echoed around the quiet clearing. "You don't get it, Leon. You're not walking away from this. You will die here."

Finally fed up, anger burned bright in his brown eyes as he stared us down. "You don't get it, Mavis. You will do what I say, or I will kill Mr. DeSalle."

"You and what fucking army?" I asked.

Instead of answering, Leon held up his hands and shot two of the biggest icicles I'd ever seen toward us.

With a yell of warning, Cam pushed me off balance, and I landed face first in a snowbank. Lifting myself as fast as I could, I turned to find Cam on the ground, bleeding from his upper arm.

"Cam!" I screamed, scrambling to him on my hands and knees.

"I'm okay, darling. It's just a flesh wound." He grinned cheekily at me. "Shame about the coat, though."

Leon walked over to stand over us. "You see, Mavis, I will kill him. Don't make this any worse for him. You want your lover to survive this, don't you?"

"Can I finish this asshole now?" I asked Cam.

His eyes drilled into mine. "Only if you can live with yourself afterward, my love."

I slowly turned toward Leon as I stood, a wicked smile on my face. "Oh, you're fucked."

Leon's smile faltered. "Mavis, wait."

But I didn't wait. The moment I felt that telltale pain in my chest, I ran for him and pushed him to the ground by his face. He seemed to fall for ages, almost as if my magic had him suspended off the field as his body quickly deteriorated before us. With a soft thump, he finally landed a split second before he was nothing more than a blood spot on the snow.

I started when I felt a hand on my shoulder. Turning to Cam, I buried my face in his uninjured shoulder. "It's over."

Familiar laughter erupted from the trees beside us, and Severin DeSalle walked into sight. My mouth dropped open as he tsked at the bloody circle in front of us. "That was completely unnecessary, ice demon. Leon was an old acquaintance of mine, a very loyal one, I might add. Now I'll have to find another idiotic demon to do my dirty work." He sighed and kicked snow over the blood before he looked up at Cam and said, "Son."

Cam didn't say a word, but I felt his grip around me tighten.

"You have nothing to say to me, Cameron?" The handsome demon chuckled to himself. "After all this madness you put me through?"

"What madness are you referring to, father?" Cam asked, his teeth clenched in rage.

He waved a hand in my direction. "The hot piece of ass you can't seem to pull your dick out of, of course. When Leon told me that he had seen you near where he thought the Exitium Daemonium had run to, I thought, how fortuitous it is that the one asset I will always have at my disposal found my missing treasure, because I knew you would turn her over to me. I had no doubt. You've always been a sniveling little suck-up to keep what little soul you had." He snarled in Cam's direction, his anger palpable. "But then I visited you, and you lied to me. To me! You lied to me just like that whore mother of yours, and I knew then, the tenuous relationship we'd forged was gone. I couldn't trust you anymore. I knew I'd have to do something, something I've always been loath to do."

Cam's face was a mixture of horror, hate, and fear as he asked, "And what is that, father?"

Severin smiled. "Get my hands dirty."

Hysterical laughter bubbled up from my throat. "Fuck you, Severin. You've done nothing but shit on your son for a century. And from the sound of it, you're planning on dragging me along with this big bag of crazy, too. But let me tell you something, fucker. It's not going to happen. I'm done being someone's secret weapon. I'm a demon, and I make my own decisions. You can either respect that, or you can meet the same fate as your underling here."

Severin stared at me for a long moment, then adjusted the ridiculously sized dick in his pants. "I will so enjoy teaching you manners, Mavis. My son may let you get away with that smart mouth, but I will find other, more creative, ways to shut you up."

"Get that thing anywhere near my mouth, and I will bite it off," I promised.

"Bite all you'd like," he said, staring openly at my breasts. "I like to play rough. And what's more, you'll like it, too."

I shuddered. "You're disgusting."

"And you, my dear, are out of time." He looked to Cam. "Say goodbye to your lover, son. She'll be fucking a real incubus from here on out."

Cameron's grip on me tightened painfully. "No."

Severin's lip curled. "What did you say to me?"

"I said no," Cam said firmly. "Leave now before you end up like Leon."

His father's laughter rang out, thick and menacing. "Was that a threat?" He laughed again. "From you?"

"You fucking heard him," I piped up. "Leave or be a spot on the snow. It's your choice."

Severin wiped tears of laughter from his eyes. "It's my choice then, is it, Mavis?"

I stood my ground, not moving. "You heard me."

With a sudden movement almost too fast to see, Severin snaked his hand around my wrist and pulled me from Cam's grasp. Wrapping his arm around my chest, he pulled me flush against his body, digging his erection painfully in my lower back.

"How is this for a choice?" he asked, tightening his hold when I fought to free myself.

"Let her go!" Cam yelled.

"No."

Panic-stricken, Cam implored me with his eyes to do what I did to Leon. His father or not, killing him was the only way I could free myself.

Nodding, I let the power engulf my hands and laid them on the arm holding me. Nothing happened.

Severin laughed again. "Fools. Who do you think had the runed device put in your chest? Do you think I'm stupid enough to come here without protection?"

Cam fell to his knees, sorrow exuding from him. "Father, please. I will do anything, anything to keep her at my side."

"Anything?" Severin asked.

"Whatever it takes," Cam said hopefully.

"Will you give me your soul?"

"No!" I screamed, fighting harder than ever. "No, Cam. You can't!"

"I have to," Cam said, unable to look at me. "I can't lose you, Mavis."

Severin's cruel voice was harsh when he spoke next. "Stand up and face me like a male of worth, Cameron. You are the son of a powerful demon. We do not cower and prostrate ourselves on the ground. And to do it over a female? There are enough females in this world to fuck a different one every night. What does one demon matter? You'll find another soon enough."

"Father, please," Cam begged, desperation tinging every word as he stood.

"Fine," Severin growled. "In return for your soul, I will give you six months to use her as you will." His grip loosened, and I stumbled forward into Cam's waiting arms. "After that, she is mine to use." He aimed an indecent smile at me. "And use her I will."

"Cam, no—" I started, but he squeezed my arm and gave me an imperceptible shake of the head to stop me.

"I'll agree to it, father."

"Very well. But know this—if you try to hide her from me, I will kill you, whether you are my only son or not. She will be mine to command."

"Yes, sir."

Severin stepped forward. "Come here, son."

Cam pushed me behind him and walked to his father, a look of absolute hatred on his face as he accepted the kiss that would mean the loss of everything that made him human. When Severin pulled back, his face was expressionless as he glanced from me to his son, then disappeared in a puff of sulfurous smoke.

EPILOGUE

*a*lone in the clearing, I stared at Cameron, horrified at what had happened.

"Why?" I asked him. "Why did you let him take it?"

"There wasn't a choice, Mavis," he said, his tone exhausted.

"Of course there was!" I shouted. "You could have chosen to keep your soul. I could've taken care of myself."

"There wasn't," he argued. "Not for me. How could I not risk everything for what we have and what you are? Do you really think I could let him take you? He's taken everything else—my freedom, my mother. I won't let him take you."

"But at what cost, Cam? Now that jackass has your soul."

He gathered me in his arms, resting his chin on top of my head. "Darling, I'm a demon. That soul wasn't going to be a ticket into some glorious afterlife. It was just holding me back."

I pulled away and met his eyes. "How?"

He grinned. "Full incubus, full powers."

"Meaning?"

"Meaning, it'll be really hard for him to find me when he doesn't know what I look like."

My jaw dropped as Cam's beautiful face and body morphed into

93

what must be an incubus's true demonic form, complete with horns, fangs, and even wings. I staggered back. "What the hell?"

In an instant, he returned to himself and grinned. "I don't think Severin realized what a gift he was handing us when he took my soul."

"No, I'm positive he didn't. Does this mean you can look like anyone?"

"Yes, I believe so. The magic is there. I can feel it."

"And we have six months to come up with a plan to defeat him."

"That's right."

I squinted at the smug, elated smile he was wearing, suspicious of what was running through his mind. "What's that grin all about?"

"I was just thinking we could continue what we were doing before we were so rudely interrupted."

I shook my head and laughed at his hopeful expression. "You are such a degenerate."

He shrugged. "I'm an incubus. It comes with the territory."

We hope you enjoyed this story in the Havenwood Falls series featuring a variety of supernatural creatures. The series is a collaborative effort by multiple authors.

Havenwood Falls books by JD Nelson:
Plans Laid Bare
Soul Laid Bare
A Demon's Redemption

Books in the Havenwood Falls Sin & Silk series:
Taming the Beast by Nadirah Foxx
Plans Laid Bare by J.D. Nelson
Shift of Fate by Victoria Escobar
Stolen Wishes by Victoria Flynn
Damned Allure by Justine Winter
Savage Salvation by Kristie Cook

Dark Seduction by Michele G. Miller & R.K. Ryals
Soul Laid Bare by J.D. Nelson
Stray With Me by E.J. Fechenda
Chase the Flames by Desiree Lafawn
Flirting With Death by Nadirah Foxx

Also try the signature line, Havenwood Falls, the historical paranormal line, Legends of Havenwood Falls, and stories from the local supernatural college in Sun & Moon Academy.

Stay up to date at www.HavenwoodFalls.com

Subscribe to our reader group and receive free stories and more!

ABOUT THE AUTHOR

JD Nelson is a bestselling author of fantasy romance and adult paranormal romance. An avid time-waster, JD enjoys watching TV and listening to audiobooks when she really should be writing.

JD loves to hear from her readers. You can contact her through her website, AuthorJDNelson.com, or on Facebook, where she spends an alarming amount of time chatting with her many author and reader friends, much to the dismay of her continually neglected manuscripts.

www.AuthorJDNelson.com

ACKNOWLEDGMENTS

Thank you to Susan Burdorf for talking me into sending in a proposal for Sin & Silk. I would have never been able to summon the courage to do it without your gentle nudge. To Danielle Bannister, I'd like to send my gratitude and a big bottle of wine for being a sounding board and listening to my petulant whining when I got discouraged. To Kristie Cook and the rest of the Havenwood Falls authors, thank you for your helpful advice and general awesomeness. You guys rock!

AN EXCERPT

~ A Havenwood Falls Sin & Silk Novella ~

HAVENWOOD FALLS

sin & silk

Shift of Fate

VICTORIA ESCOBAR

Shift of Fate (**A Havenwood Falls Sin & Silk Novella**) **by Victoria Escobar**

Audrey Smith has never had a place to call home, living as a nomad because of what she is and what she's not. A shifter without a shift, she doesn't belong with a pride, but she's too much "other" to blend in with humans. Her last attempt turned her into a science project. And finding a mate? Forget about it. She'd always been told she wasn't shifter enough for it to happen.

When Audrey totals her car and awakens in Havenwood Falls, she immediately makes plans to leave. But the sexier-than-sin paramedic who pulled her from the wreckage has other ideas, claiming her as his. But based on everything she knows, that's impossible.

Nicholas Jordan never expected to find his mate and settle down. If she lived in Havenwood Falls, he would have met her already. Then Audrey literally crashes into his life. Not only does he want her, but he *needs* her. She belongs to him, and he to her.

Accepting Nicholas's claim would betray everything Audrey's ever believed about herself. But the longer she denies the mating bond, the more dangerous it becomes for them both, putting their lives—and the pride's future—at risk.

SHIFT OF FATE

AUDREY

The Challenger roared down the winding highway of Colorado. The gas light wasn't on yet, but the time of reckoning would soon be at hand. Skipping a break in the last town proved to be a worse idea with each dark, sign-less mile.

"Audrey, you're a fucking idiot." If I had more sense, I'd turn the car around before there was no chance of making it back. Something visceral possessed me to keep going farther, faster, without stopping. All roads went somewhere, after all—even the dark, empty ones.

When the night terrors returned two days ago, I packed everything I owned—which wasn't much—and left Iowa. The longer the delay, the more the terrors would seep into daily life, and paranoia would eat at my sanity. Been there, done that, and it wasn't pretty or pleasant to think I was crazy.

So I left and drove. Hopefully far enough to leave the terrors behind. For a time. The cycle would eventually start anew, but for a while, I hoped for a pretense of peace.

Stopping would be required soon, though. A body, even one with perks like mine, needed rest and real food to survive. If I went another twenty-four hours without sleep, I might drive my junkyard rescue right off the edge of one of these winding roads. A few years ago, that wouldn't have sounded as scary as it did now.

I leaned over the steering wheel and squinted into the distance. The moonless sky made the dark wilderness somehow darker. The clouds covering the starlight added depth to the darkness, making it appear more like the pit of some abyss than a night-shrouded forest.

There had to be something out here. A homestead, or a cabin. A ski lodge even. I could pay for a room, and maybe talk to someone about gasoline. Even pay to use someone's spare gas can. Anything was better than ending up empty on the side of the road in the middle of nowhere. Especially since I wasn't sure where the road went.

Trees vanished into the horizon all around without showing any promise of civilization. Not even a dirt road that could lead to some recluse's cabin. I loved the wild, but the civilized part of me needed indoor plumbing and hot water heaters. The very thought of a warm bath made my tired eyes flutter closed.

The sudden blast of a new song on the radio jolted me upright. I shook my head and reached for the window to let in some of the cold air. Maybe the icy November chill would keep me awake long enough to reach some kind of destination.

Movement drew my attention back to the road.

"Fuck." I had enough time to register the ghostly looking deer in the road before I hit it and the car spun crazily out of control.

Metal ground against metal, and the noise terrified me. The air bag didn't go off as I threw my hands up to protect my face from the flying glass of the shattered windshield. When the vehicle pinged off the guard rail, my head smashed into the steering wheel. I saw stars in a very literal sense. In seconds, the car came to a sudden, neck-breaking halt in the middle of the road.

My normally crisp vision blurred and spotted; no amount of blinking cleared it. I could smell blood, oil, and gasoline. I tried moving, only to bite my lip against a scream when pain flared throughout my body. Until rescue came, I was stuck. I prayed the car wasn't on fire somewhere.

Would someone come by and see, or would I die on the unnamed road? I closed my eyes and hoped for rescue but waited for death.

NICHOLAS

I was only in bed for twenty minutes when the message came through about a car accident on the very edge of the town's border. Instead of bitching about the ungodly hour, I climbed out of bed, dressed, and went out to do my job, calling Liam Peters on the way.

The city was either too cheap or too poor to hire on additional EMTs, but I never questioned it. Job security and all. Liam was a volunteer firefighter with an EMT certification, which made him more valuable than most of the others that took shifts with me. He met me at the ambulance bay of the fire station, wearing his usual sunglasses and carrying coffee.

My jaw cracked as I stifled a yawn. Since getting the paramedic certification a couple of months ago, I'd been busier. There was something nice about being the only certified paramedic in town, but at the same time, it fucked with sleep and anything else normal. I hoped a couple of the graduating high school kids would take the request for EMTs seriously, but I wasn't holding my breath.

If I was lucky, there wouldn't be much to do, the car's occupants would be dead, and I'd get another few hours of sleep before heading to the gym. Since my best friend Braden McCabe died, I made sure to hit the gym at least once a day. I wasn't an alpha, but I'd be damned if I would ever be too weak to save a friend's life again.

"That doesn't look pretty." Liam leaned forward in the seat.

I shifted the ambulance a little so I could see around the slowing tow truck. A whistle cut the air as I got a glimpse of the mangled car. "Elk, you think?"

Liam cocked his head. "Possibly. Only other thing I can think of that damn big is a bear."

My hand ran through my long fringe of hair, which reminded me —I needed a cut. Another thing to add to my list of shit to do when I found time. "Let's see if anyone's alive."

I pulled the ambulance off to the shoulder and climbed out, zipping up my blue work jacket with the bright silver reflective EMS on the back and "JORDAN" written across the left breast. I grabbed the medic box before slamming the door and heading over to the crash.

Shame about the car. The classic, while needing a paint job, was still a dream car for most. Probably some crazy-ass wannabe street racer. Stupid too, to be racing down the county road in the middle of the damn night.

Deputy Conall stood next to the driver's side—what was left of it —while Sheriff Ric Kasun leaned in through the crushed windshield. Conall directed a flashlight in through the mangled windshield. Even with the poor light of not quite dawn, both shifter men should have been able to see fine, but as a cat shifter, I didn't question them and risk a pissing match.

"Liam, Nicholas." Ric pulled his broad body out of the crash. "The girl's breathing, but I can't tell you the extent of the injuries. Joshua." Ric moved away from the crash to have a few words with the mechanic, who already had the tow truck in place.

"Should have brought a metalworker," I muttered, as Liam tried to find a delicate way of reaching the driver. I stepped up to the driver's window, but thanks to the collapsed pillar, I could barely get a hand in. I glanced across and then stood up to look at the other side. "Passenger side looks relatively undamaged."

Liam went around to the other side. He glanced at me as he tried the handle. "Door's locked."

I lifted a brow.

He shrugged and stuck his elbow through the window. "Door's open."

Liam slid into the passenger seat, not even bothered by the newly broken glass. He placed a hand on the girl's head and looked down at the pedals. "Wheel well is collapsed. Looks like her leg could be stuck. She's flirting with death."

"Let's see about getting her out and to the med center."

Liam climbed out of the car. "You're smaller than I am. You get in there and pull her out."

I snorted. "By what, two inches?"

"Wide, ass wipe. Despite your gym hours, you're still scrawny."

"Like fucking hell I am." But I moved into position and slid into the car. "Get the damn stretcher."

Her seatbelt was still firmly in place and the first thing I had to deal with. At least the girl was smart enough to be wearing it. Too often I got called out and the seatbelt hadn't been able to do its job.

I angled her so she would fall against my chest when I cut the strap. My safety tool sliced the belt like cutting butter. Her weight didn't even register when she tipped, and it brought a frown to my face. For her height—she was nearly as tall as me—she was too light.

With her face tilted toward the light, I could see sharp angles in her cheeks and a pallor to her skin that shouted malnutrition. My fingers ghosted over her cheek, careful of the bruises. Her lashes fluttered, and for a frozen moment in time, her molten gold gaze stared into my eyes.

Mine.

The unexpected claim slammed into me as hard as the elk had her car. All my muscles tensed. I fought a small battle with myself to stay calm and not lose my damn mind. She was injured, for fuck's sake.

The damn cat inside me took notice, and I forced my gaze away, closing my eyes. There was a time and a place—and this sure as hell wasn't it.

"Jordan, what's taking so long?" Liam tapped the hood next to my head. His head tipped just enough to let me know he noticed. The hellhound was perceptive as fuck.

"Yeah, yeah." I shifted under his scrutiny and returned my attention to where the woman's feet should be. She whimpered a bit when I tried to pull her free, but didn't regain consciousness. "Her left foot is stuck, and she's bleeding from her right leg. By the bruising, she's likely concussed as well."

"Let me get some help over here." Liam stepped away and flagged down Ric and Joshua.

I took a chance and glanced down at the woman again, but this time her eyes were closed. Dried blood crusted along her golden hairline and marred her temple. Her shoulder looked out of place . . . but she did otherwise look in one piece. My major concern now was getting her—my mate—out of the vehicle. Fate had a fucking twisted sense of humor.

$\sim$

AUDREY

Pain entered my consciousness before anything else. Everything hurt. No amount of subtle shifting relieved it.

When I forced my eyes open, the ceiling above my head didn't have the familiar pattern of water stains in my room. I flailed into an upright position, with my heart pounding in my ears before the memory of the accident came back. I wasn't in Iowa anymore.

I rolled a shoulder and winced at the pain that radiated down to my fingertips. Motion from the left caught my eye. I froze.

An old man sat in a chair positioned in front of a curtain, with a book in hand. His eyes reminded me of ice storms in Montana, and I waited as their frosty blue gaze studied me. "Finally awake."

"How long have I been out?" I noted my back and neck hurt almost as much as my shoulder when I shifted in his direction. I racked my memory, trying to put the pieces back together.

I was nearly sure he wasn't the man who pulled me out of my car. He was too old to be doing rescue work, even though the intensity of his stare spoke volumes of his authority. The cane leaning against his chair added to the elderly visage.

"If you passed out immediately after the accident, then around sixteen hours. With the bump on your head, no one was sure if or when you would wake up." He stood, sliding the book into his pocket and grabbing his cane. "I'm Elsmed Fairchild. Welcome to Havenwood Falls."

"Havenwood Falls? I'm still in Colorado, right?" I rolled my pained shoulder a second time and grimaced as the bite went deep.

"You are. Where are you from?" He stepped up to the side of the bed, and I did my best to avoid his deep, soul-burning gaze.

"I'm driving from Iowa. Or I was." I grimaced as I attempted to find a comfortable sitting position. "I haven't hurt this bad in a while."

"You're lucky you're alive, really. Mule deer wouldn't have caused that kind of damage. The sheriff is assuming it's an elk, though no one has come forward with the kill. What was in Iowa, if I may ask?"

"Nothing important enough to keep me there." Giving up, I flopped back in the bed and closed my eyes. I wish I had something to deal with the deep aching.

"I'll call the nurse in and get you something for the pain in a moment."

I didn't voice how creepy it was he seemed to have read my mind. "Do you sit in on all accident patients who are unconscious?"

"Only the supernatural ones."

My eyes shot open and darted to his face. "Mr. Fairchild, I'm not supernatural."

The denial was automatic. I didn't pretend to not know what he talked about. There was something preternatural about his demeanor that said he wouldn't take bullshit. Even as old as he was.

"Yet you're not denying they exist, as most normal humans would. Your shift is there in your mind, but her presence is faint, almost as if she is covered, or blocked somehow." Mr. Fairchild shook his head. "It's not something that needs immediate attention."

I shifted, uncomfortable with the topic, as I always was when someone asked about it. "When can I leave?"

"Dr. Underwood mentioned something about a concussion. Now that you're awake, they'll likely be able to address that. Probably some kind of observation."

"Oh."

"I haven't left Havenwood Falls in some years. Tell me, do they talk about the Collector outside our little canyon?"

"Collector of what? There are all sorts of collectors in Denver. I met a dragon in Chicago that liked to collect shifter pelts. I didn't stay there long. Do you know what happened to my car?"

Mr. Fairchild pursed his lips a moment before speaking. "Joshua runs the tow company for Havenwood Falls. You'll want to talk to him, most likely."

"Oh, okay." I closed my eyes again, suddenly swamped by a wave of fatigue.

"I must inform you, there are rules for supernaturals here. I'm sure you'll understand in time. Due to current events in town, you'll need to be registered before you can leave the medical center. For your safety as much as the town's. Adelaide will come and discuss all that with you tomorrow."

Registered? I fought to stay awake enough to process the words. "But I don't have a shift."

"Knowledge is power, Ms. Smith. Never forget that. I'll fetch a nurse for you."

"Thank you." I clenched my jaw to keep from yawning. The voices outside the curtain faded into a dull murmur that reminded me of a stream's trickle as I drifted between wakefulness and sleep.

My mind lingered on Elsmed Fairchild a moment. What a strange individual. He felt powerful without looking it. As I drifted off to sleep, I realized he had said my name without me giving it to him. What kind of town was Havenwood Falls?

∾

NICHOLAS

My parents have always been the rock in the storm of my life. Whenever I needed help—whether it be physical, like replacing the roof on my cabin, or emotional, dealing with the grief of Braden's passing—they were there. They made it clear when I was a child they would always have my back, and they had never let me down.

The drive through Creekwood wasn't long enough to put my

thoughts in order. Tension followed me from the day before, and I hoped they'd provide a solution. My parents had always hoped I'd settle down with a nice local girl, regardless of supernatural status. A stranger from out of town, whose name I didn't even know, wasn't what I'd been expecting. Not that I really had been expecting anything at all. I enjoyed my bachelor life, and at thirty, still had plenty of years ahead of me to settle down.

I didn't knock on the door of my childhood home. If my parents weren't home, I'd have to say something to them about the fact I didn't have to use my key to get in. Despite crime being relatively low, there was no point in encouraging the temptation.

The familiarity of the house washed over me when I stepped in, but did nothing to relieve my tension. "Mom? Dad?"

"In the office, honey."

I followed Mom's shout to the office, where I found both my parents. Dad sat behind the desk, and Mom sat in the lounge chair thing by the bookcase. A book lay in Mom's lap; she liked Dad's company even if they didn't say a word to each other.

I pulled out the leather chair and sat down in it, but immediately stood and paced. There was no way I could sit at a time like this.

"Shouldn't my favorite son be at work?" Mom grinned and winked.

"I could say the same of my mother. My reports are caught up, and the station is clean." I rolled my shoulders, suddenly uncomfortable with the topic I wanted to bring up. "I didn't come to talk about work."

Mom canted her head. "Hoping for an easy meal? You're welcome to come for dinner tonight."

"It's not that either, though I appreciate the offer."

Dad looked away from his monitor and at me. "What do you need, Nicholas?"

My hand ran over my still-too-long hair. I'd stop at the barber after this. "I've met my mate—I think."

Mom sat up. "You think?"

Dad folded his hands in the *don't bullshit a bullshitter* pose of my youth. "Mates either are or aren't, son. There's no in between."

"I know that. You don't think I know that?" I walked over to the liquor cabinet in the corner and looked for something to pour.

"It's a little early—" Dad cut off.

"What happened, Nicholas?" Mom's voice was soft as I poured a scotch.

I tossed it back before answering her. "I had a rescue yesterday morning. Car accident. And don't start about the falling in love with the rescued shit. I took the classes. I know the deal. Why do you think I waited a day?" I poured another drink. The scotch wouldn't get me drunk—at least, not for long. Now if I tapped into Dad's bottle of Fey Spirits . . .

"So you went on a rescue?" Dad leaned back in his chair.

"Ten seconds, maybe. I had ten seconds of eye contact." The second drink went down as smoothly as the first. I faced my parents. "How did you know? That you belonged to each other?"

"It's visceral, Nicholas. Tell us how you feel." Mom set her book aside.

"Tense. There's an energy I can't burn off, and I've tried. Restless, anxious, unsettled." I began pacing again. "There's no reason to be this way. I don't even know the girl's name."

"What's stopping you from finding out?" Dad's eyes followed my movement.

"She's unconscious. Or was, when I took her in. I lingered when Dr. Underwood went in to look at her. Concussion. Dislocated shoulder. Fractured two ribs—where the seatbelt held her in place. Sprained ankle that would heal faster if it was actually broken instead. Honestly, she's damn lucky to be alive."

"Is she a shifter?" Mom asked.

I shrugged. "Smelled like a cat. Couldn't tell you what kind." I shoved both my hands in my hair and pulled. "I feel like I should be doing something, but don't know what that is. There's this . . . thing. It feels like it's pushing, but I have no fucking idea where or why."

"Start small." Dad gestured to the door. "You know she's

unconscious, but was in a car accident. Do the things she can't do for herself at the moment. Where are her things? Has the insurance been contacted?"

"Does she have toiletries and items to clean up with when she wakes up?" Mom added.

"What's that supposed to do?" I stared at them both. They'd lost their minds. How were menial tasks supposed to identify this girl as a mate?

"It gives you time to figure out what you feel, and gives you vague insight to her life before the accident." Mom gave me a pointed look. "Only you can determine if this girl is your mate or not. If she is, you'll know."

"How? That's what I came to you for. How will I know? How did you know?" I glared from one to the other. "You're not going to help at all?"

Dad sighed. "We are helping, but we're not going to hold your hand through it. You're a grown, respectable man, and I couldn't ask for a finer son. However, if you can't figure out the basics of a mate, then somewhere along the line, I failed as a father."

"You haven't failed, Dad. I just . . ."

"It's scary and new." Mom stood and wrapped me in a hug. "You've always been so sure, and then when Braden died, you used your grief to become the best man you can be. But you never questioned the path you walked. Now you're uncertain. Flailing in the unknown. Take our advice. Go, do for her what she can't do for herself. And go visit Rose at Howe's. Ask her for the soaps and such that I get from her. A shifter woman would appreciate the gently scented items."

I sighed and hugged Mom back. "I don't want to go about this the wrong way."

"You can only be who you are, Nicholas. Trust in fate." She kissed my cheek and pulled away. "Shoo. Your father has paperwork to finish."

"Thanks." The dismissal stung, especially when it felt like they hadn't provided any information at all, but I did as asked. They wouldn't provide anything else even if I camped in the office with them.

The only thing I could do was follow instructions. Joshua towed the car; he likely had all her things. As far as starting points went, it was better than anything else I could think of. Since Howe's was around the corner from the garage, it wouldn't hurt to stop there too.

Purchase *Shift of Fate* wherever books are sold.

www.ingramcontent.com/pod-product-compliance
Lightning Source LLC
Chambersburg PA
CBHW052006170626
46808CB00007B/2804